DANIEL SANTOS

GRAVE OF
LOST DREAMS
DOWNPOUR

Contents

1. Chapter 1   1

2. September 12th   8

3. Chapter 2   9

4. September 13th   20

5. Chapter 3   21

6. September 15th   31

7. Chapter 4   32

8. September 16th   42

9. Chapter 5   43

10. September 17th   50

11. Chapter 6   51

12. December 13th   57

13. Chapter 7   58

14. December 15th   65

15.	Chapter 8	66
16.	January 3rd	78
17.	Chapter 9	79
18.	January 5th	84
19.	Chapter 10	85
20.	January 12th	87
21.	Chapter 11	88
22.	February 14th	95
23.	Chapter 12	97
24.	February 16th	104
25.	Chapter 13	105
26.	????	112
27.	Chapter 14	113
28.	???	119
29.	Chapter 15	120
30.	Chapter 16	124
31.	Chapter 17	131
32.	Chapter 18	138
33.	Chapter 19	142
34.	Chapter 20	147
35.	Chapter 21	154
36.	Chapter 22	162
37.	Chapter 23	166
38.	Chapter 24	174

39. Chapter 24   179

40. Chapter 40   186

Chapter 1

PRESENT

Patrick leaned over the railing, casting his shadow over the cliff as the sun slowly rose above the orange clouds. He'd been driving since the dead of night when fog shrouded his vision. Even with his high beams activated, the weather still acted as a veil to conceal the world, but as dawn broke, as the clouds gave way to the sun, he found himself in a whole new world. The sudden sight of the vast ocean and the stench of nearby fishing huts reminded him he was no longer in Iowa. He let out a deep breath that hung in the air.

If only you were here.

Patrick breathed heavily into his cupped hands. Years ago, he stood in this very state of Alaska, traversing the small city of Skagway. Except at the time, his brother accompanied him rather than the unbearable weight of guilt.

Together, they would listen to the blaring horn of cruise ships docked by the shore, but this time, only the harsh winds broke the sound barrier. With the ferry long gone and his rental car now his only method of travel, the air suddenly felt like a heavy blanket, wrapping him into a cocoon. He glanced over his shoulder at the empty parking lot, where the vehicle waited for him, a pile of clothes in the passenger seat. His hands squeezed the railing tightly until the frozen metal stung his skin as a minor form of punishment. Four years ago, he promised himself to get over his little brother's death. But no matter what he told himself, he still clung onto him.

"We're back, Delan," he whispered, thinking about their last trip. Patrick returned his attention to the ocean and retrieved his brother's journal from his pocket. Most of it was ramblings about Skagway, but the memories contained within those words urged him to visit the place.

In my dreams, Patrick and I are riding the ziplines through the trees once again. Just like we did seven years ago. He promised we'd go there again, but I'm thinking that was all talk. Just the ramblings of my older brother. After all, he was ten. What ten-year-old can make such big promises?

The sight of Delan's handwriting pulled on his heart. Patrick traced his fingers over the ebony ink and smiled. Despite the pain, there was no denying the massive impact each line of writing made on him. "I'm sorry. I couldn't keep my promise." A stabbing sensation poked at his chest, reminding him how disappointed he was in himself for acting like a lunatic. Initially, he chalked up his small comments to Delan as a regular coping mechanism, but when they evolved into full blown conversations, he knew he was entering dangerous mental territory.

Patrick returned to his car, only to sit in the driver's seat and talk to the pile of his brother's clothes. "I can't remember how long it's been. Isn't that silly? How can I forget our vacation here?" Patrick shut the journal gently, put it in his pocket and pulled out his phone. During the latter half of his senior year, he procrastinated for hours at a time by listening to one of his favorite creators on the internet. Luckily for him, he received a Wi-Fi signal despite his remote location. He scrolled through his video feed until he finally arrived at the woman he listened to almost every day.

He tapped on the thumbnail that depicted her light skin and dyed black hair. Upon starting the video, he spun up the volume.

"Hey guys, it's me, Sofia. I just wanted to give you an update on my writing. You guys already know it. It's the one with the abandoned ghost town." Patrick smiled as he listened. At first, he never took much of an interest in reading, but Delan was the complete opposite. As Delan had droned on and on about his hobby, Patrick tried it, landing him on Sofia's channel.

"I can't believe I'm actually excited to read a new book."

He smiled at the stack of clothes before completely reclining the car seat.

"The biggest update I wanted to share with you all is my book cover!" announced Sofia.

Patrick watched the video transition into an image of two enormous towers caught in a snowy town.

But just as Patrick was becoming invested in the cover art reveal, the Wi-Fi slowed down, sending the video spiraling into a lengthy buffer. The audio cut in and out until eventually, the content paused entirely. He slapped his phone on the side while letting out a quiet cuss. The video skipped a few frames.

"As you can see the main character, Amber—"

The video stalled again, stuck on a still frame of Sofia holding her laptop in front of the camera to display her story cover.

Patrick shook his head, wishing he could see the rest of it instead of only the left hemisphere depicting the main character and half of a tower. He tossed his phone onto the seat next to him and leaned forward with his arms resting on the wheel.

Stupid, he thought to himself. Patrick grunted and punched the air-conditioning vent. The strike stung his knuckles. A tiny cut appeared across his skin. *Another outburst.* He ground his teeth together and shut his eyes to listen to the waves. His ears fought to relax into the ambience surrounding him, but with each passing second, the memories of Delan pushed him to the brink. He saw his brother smiling as he flew down the zipline, and the way his eyes lit up at the ice cream shop.

Not right now. Patrick clenched and unclenched his fist, forcing his mind to stay within the present moment. *The waves. Listen to the waves.*

But just as his hands ceased trembling, lighting struck in the distance. He tried to keep his eyes shut, only to lose focus when the heavy patter of rain overtook everything. He looked out his window toward the lonely gas station. The water soaked the pumps, while the building itself acted as one bright beacon. Patrick pursed his lips as he tried to imagine who waited inside.

A man with a wife. Maybe he has a child, or even a sibling. What if it's not a man? It could be a woman. Patrick dropped his head on top of the steering wheel. *I need to talk to people again.* He drifted his sight to the clothes in the seat beside him.

"Sorry to leave you," he said, stepping out of the car. The pile echoed a sense of guilt. He whistled a tune, softly as he approached the building. Once inside, the bell above the entrance rang.

"Hello?" he said aloud, but received no response. Patrick darted his head around the shelves, only to realize no one waited behind the till. Instead, the light above the register shone down on the empty counter. Small particles of dust lingered in the air like locusts.

No matter how empty the store was, it appeared to be in service. Looking around, the pumps were relatively clean; the power was on, and a freshly used mop stood in the corner. Patrick perused the shelves to pass the time, figuring an employee would come around. Knowing that Skagway prized itself on tourism, he figured he'd have plenty of interesting things to see. His eyes scanned each product, expecting to find a mug or keychain, depicting a salmon or having the name 'Skagway' etched into it, but much to his disappointment, everything looked the same as the convenience stores in his hometown. He turned his attention to another shelf and flipped through an assortment of magazines. He grumbled "*nonsense,*" underneath his breath until deciding it was foolish to plan an entire conversation with the employee. After all, it would be impossible to know the exact words someone says. "Just talk," he told himself. But the more he thought about making conversation with the first person he saw, the more his heart fluttered. He lifted his wrist to view his watch. So far, ten minutes passed since he pulled into the parking lot. He sunk his tooth into the inside of his cheek. *Why isn't anyone here?*

Patrick kept fingering through the endless stack until his cheeks turned red. Whatever he found certainly wasn't a regular piece of literature. Instead, it seemed more like one of those old *Playboy* magazines he found in his dad's drawer. Suddenly, the urge to wash his hands overwhelmed him. Even though he couldn't shake off the question of why such magazines were stocked here given the internet's prominence, he still understood their appeal.

Now he felt thankful no one was around. Otherwise, he'd look like some sort of pervert. Patrick tapped his foot against the tiled floor, trying to regain his composure. "Who's there?" he asked, when the bell rang again. A white furry coat closed in on his ankles. He looked down and spotted a Siberian Husky sniffing his shoes. The animal let out a short whimper as he tried to get Patrick's attention.

"This sucks, right?" he said, alluding to the isolation. He reached out to scratch its neck, making the dog vigorously wag its tail. Patrick examined the nametag dangling below the collar. "Charlie. That's your name?" The animal let out a bark before letting his tongue hang downward like an apple ready to fall out of a tree. Charlie shut his eyes and nuzzled his nose against Patrick's shin. "My brother loved dogs," Patrick said with a weak smile. He tried to run his fingers through his thick coat, but Charlie turned around and sprinted away. Patrick watched him disappear down the road. "Stay safe," he whispered.

From then, Patrick returned to the register with the magazine in hand. He rotated his head to scan the room as though he were about to commit a crime. Despite his mind telling him "*no,*" he retrieved a few bills from his pocket, leaving about one dollar more than what the magazine cost. Patrick looked at the black camera hanging above him and waved the money in the air.

"It's a ten and one five," he said, slightly quieter than usual as the disgust from his perverted mind set in. Afterward, he left the store and hurried through the rain shower. He kept his head low and avoided eye contact with his brother's clothes.

"Sorry, it took so long," he said after entering the vehicle. Patrick took off his hoodie and gently tossed it over the pile. "This isn't for you." He began thumbing through each page while keeping his nose buried in the images. *Shouldn't I like this stuff?* He pursed his lips together as he tried to convince himself to become excited. But no matter what, not a single picture made Patrick feel anything other than dread. Whether it be one beautiful blonde woman with light skin or the dark-haired woman with softer features, none of it made him happy. In fact, all he ever felt was a gnawing feeling in his chest, telling him that this wasn't what he wanted. But why didn't he want it? Patrick pursed his lips, telling himself, "It was just one wicked woman . . ." His voice trailed away as he thought back to his senior year of high school. Despite four years passing, he couldn't let go of the one person who made him even more confused than he already was.

Patrick sighed, shut the pages, and cursed himself for being so unsure of who he really was. *Fifteen dollars wasted.* He shook his head and tapped his fingertips on the steering wheel. The rain slowly gathered more strength, preparing to turn into a storm. *What kind of person am I?* Patrick looked down at the cover, wondering if perhaps the woman on the front page would make him happier. His eyes glazed over it, capturing everything from her darker skin tone to the underwear she wore. Despite that, everything felt wrong. For a second, he wondered how he'd feel if it was a man on the cover, like one of those Chippendale shows in Las Vegas. However, nothing changed. The mental torment lingered, putting him more on edge. "What the fuck is wrong with me!" he screamed, and chucked the lewd publication onto the dashboard. "Fuck! Fuck!" He slapped his palm onto the steering wheel, sending a flurry of blaring horns with each strike.

God, is nothing ever going to go my way? He put a hand to his stomach, feeling a stirring in the deepest recesses of it. "Please excuse my language," he whispered. Patrick pulled down his hoodie and straightened the stack of his brother's clothes.

September 12th

My Special and Extremely Awesome Journal

High school doesn't feel that different. My friends are still here and so is everyone I know. We just look older and more tired, but that's about it. Well, that and the fact that I see Patrick now and then. But he has 'second' lunch period, so we never get to sit together. But even if we had the same lunch period, would he eat with me? I've always gotten the impression that social hierarchies exist, but I don't see that at all. Everyone is just trying to get through the day. It's nothing like those high school movies I see, but then again, those came out in the early 2000s, so maybe things have changed since then. I mean, those times are long behind us. I guess times have changed or were they never that way? Oh whatever, Ms. Hawthorne is a movie buff, plus she's, I think she's, still young, so maybe she was in high school during those times.

Chapter 2

PAST

Patrick waited outside the front entrance of his high school, basking in the warm air of spring. He closed his eyes and gave a sigh of satisfaction as the sunrays kissed his face. The warmth gave way to a sense of euphoria, making the wait more tolerable than the previous semester.

"Hey," a voice said. Patrick opened his eyes, only to see Khen standing next to him. "You're waiting for Delan again?" The boy smirked, revealing a huge grin beneath his long hair.

Patrick nodded. "What do you think he did this time?"

"Don't know. It's not like he tells me either."

Patrick sat on the nearest bench and leaned forward. He ran his fingers through his hair, wondering if it looked just as good as Khen's. His moment of insecurity deepened when he realized he still hadn't grown any facial hair. When his mouth turned into a frown, Khen slowly chuckled.

"What?" Patrick asked, annoyed.

"Nothing."

Patrick eyed him longer, which only made Khen's struggle to maintain his composure even more obvious.

"What the heck is going on in your head?"

Khen patted him on the shoulder. "You just look like one of my aunts with your bare face!"

"What?"

Without speaking another word, Khen pulled out his phone to reveal the picture of a woman in traditional Japanese attire covering her mouth with one hand. "I forgot what place she worked at. But she had to do this all the time for one play she performed in."

"Maybe I'll never age. just like her," Patrick said with a smirk, thinking he made a good point. Especially since Khen's aunt looked the same as she did when Patrick met her during his elementary school days.

"Yeah, but don't you want to look older? More mature?"

Patrick shook his head, cursing the men in his family for appearing too feminine. "Can't you just leave?"

Khen gave him an odd look. "What? You don't want me here anymore? Eleven years together and a bad joke is all it takes to throw me away?"

"It's not that I don't want you here. I'm just stressed about having to deal with Delan all the time. My brother never gets in trouble, but for two months, Ms. Hawthorne's been giving him detention almost every day."

Khen scoffed at him. "Whatever you say. At least Delan never stopped having fun."

Patrick gave him a side eye. "What do you mean?"

"'*What do you mean?*'" Khen asked sarcastically. "Remember all those times I came over to your house to play games? We stayed up until five in the morning! Now, you won't even stay up past ten!"

"Well, I'm sorry, but my mom is a lot stricter than yours," Patrick scoffed, and folded his arms. He sank deeper into the bench with his eyes gazing into the distance.

"Can't you stop acting so sad? I want my old friend back," Khen sighed, and stared at Patrick, but rather than responding, Patrick only nodded his head, unsure of what to make of everything.

"I'm sorry," he said with an exasperated breath. Khen shoved his hands in his pockets and silently walked away. "How about we talk later? I'll log onto my computer, and we can play a game!" Patrick yelled at his back.

Even though Khen didn't turn around, the slight rise in his shoulders told Patrick that he heard him. Patrick closed his eyes and took in a deep breath, wondering if Khen was right. Had he really lost himself these past few years? He watched Khen make his way further into the parking lot. His confident demeanor exuded a commanding presence, one that only seemed to develop after they left middle school. But unlike Khen, Patrick would practically waddle down the hallways. He turned on his phone camera to look at himself. He ran his fingers over his chin, wishing he could draw a beard, while he pinched his cheeks, praying one day he'd lose the little bits of fat within it.

If only.

He slumped his shoulders, trying hard to accept that he may never look the way he wanted to. Soon, he eyed his arms, realizing that he needed to eat more. *Too scrawny.* Afterward, he looked to the window that was covered by a curtain. He knew that's where Ms. Hawthorne's class was. After all, during his freshman year, Patrick was sitting in the same room, struggling with the same schoolwork Delan was doing. Still, back then, the curtain was never kept shut. Only when Delan started having his cluster headaches did he beg her to keep the room dark. Suddenly, a breeze formed, quickly picking up speed, and reminding him how volatile the weather of the Midwest can be.

"Damn it," he whispered. Patrick hugged himself tightly, cursing his brother for running so late. He stared enviously at the other students boarding the buses. If only those yellow tubes stayed a little longer, then Delan could hop on one of them rather than hitching a ride in Patrick's car. After a few more seconds of sulking, Patrick heard the metal legs of a chair scratching the floor. The sound originated from Ms. Hawthorne's classroom, but nothing else happened afterward. Patrick looked at his wristwatch, realizing that about forty-five minutes had passed since the school bell rang.

He stared at the front doors, expecting Delan to burst through at any moment. Patrick quickly slung his backpack over his shoulder and fidgeted with his car keys. But when his brother failed to show up, Patrick marched toward the doors.

"Delan, get over here!" The young boy stood by the entrance in a zombie-like state with his black hair frazzled and coat wrinkled. "Listen, I'm sick of having to stay late for you! "Why don't—" Patrick immediately clamped his mouth shut and sniffed the air.

Delan averted his gaze. "Let's just leave," he mumbled. Patrick glared at him, slowly leaning closer until he realized the smell was radiating off Delan's shirt.

"Either you're just as fruity as that perfume or you've got a girlfriend. Which is it?" Patrick asked with a sly grin.

"Move." Delan pushed Patrick against the door frame as he left the building.

"You don't have to hide it!" Patrick called out to him. He picked up the pace as he tried to catch up with Delan. Soon, they both found themselves in the parking lot. "Have you been staying up late talking to this girl? Maybe you're getting detention because you've been falling asleep in class?" When they finally reached the car, Patrick folded his arms across his chest and leaned against the passenger side door. Delan looked up at him with a sharp glare.

"Let's go home."

"Not until you answer me." For a moment, the brothers stared at each other, with neither one breaking eye contact.

"Move." Delan gripped Patrick's arm, but Patrick refused to budge. "There's no need to be shy about it. We always share our secrets with each other. We've been doing that since we were kids."

Delan sighed. "No, I don't have a girlfriend." He spoke bluntly, but Patrick didn't buy into it. The telltale signs of Delan's deceit became obvious to him over the years. And judging by the slight fall in his brother's pitch followed by the faint eye twitch, told Patrick that he was lying, and another staring contest ensued.

"Wait a minute," Patrick said. He reached out and yanked his brother forward by the shirt collar. "Jesus, mom is going to kill you!" He pulled down Delan's shirt collar just enough to reveal the bruise on the side of his neck. "Love bites and perfume? Can't you be more discreet?"

"Why should you care?" Delan shoved his shoulder into Patrick, forcing him to step aside. When the boy finally got inside the car, Patrick grabbed the handle before his brother could shut it.

"Listen, it's not the hickey itself that bothers me. What bothers me is that I'll be in trouble too. The moment mom sees that, she'll go ballistic and then I'll get grounded because I'm supposed to look after you!"

"That's your problem!" Delan pulled on the door, trying to resist Patrick's strength, but he never wavered.

"But it is my problem. If you're in trouble, I'm in trouble."

"Just leave me alone!" Delan shoved his heel into Patrick's thigh, making him lose his grip. Once he shut himself in the car, Patrick grunted and went to the driver's seat.

"Just do whatever you can to avoid getting caught," he said sternly. Patrick firmly planted himself in his seat, letting his engine rev as he started the car. He let it run a little longer than usual, garnering a long stare from Delan.

"Can't you just drive home?" he asked.

But Patrick grinned as he tuned in to his engine.

"No."

His mind went back to Khen and the way he revved his car to impress their peers. Patrick imagined his schoolmates stopping by to watch him. He pictured the faces of the other guys as they complimented his vehicle, or the prettiest girls in his class who he could take for a drive. But his fantasy ended when he realized the car was rolling backward.

"What the hell? Are you trying to kill us!"

Patrick slapped Delan's hand away from the hand brake.

"If you pulled out of the parking lot, I wouldn't have done that."

Patrick sighed and shook his head. He glanced at his brother after pulling out of the parking lot. As the school faded away into the distance, he thought more about Khen and how he could be just like him. He turned up the heater to where sweat formed around his wrist, and out of the corner of his eye, Delan wafted the air in front of him.

"I swear, you're one of those people who turns the knob all the way to the left when you're in the shower," Delan complained while taking his coat off. The sight of his little brother's face contorting in pure discomfort made Patrick feel a strong sense of displeasure. For a moment, he reflected on the past few minutes until the introspection caused physical pain.

"Okay, I'm sorry." He lessened the heat.

"Thank you." Delan turned his head to stare out the window, while Patrick tried to make small talk.

"So, how's detention?" he asked awkwardly.

"It's detention. I don't know what'd you expect me to say."

Right. Patrick whistled the same tune their mother used to lull them to sleep, hoping to catch Delan's attention, but unlike before, he simply ignored the music. "Remember that? Mom used to sing it to us."

"Yeah." He spoke dispassionately. "And she used to be nice to us, and you used to be nice to me." The last phrase felt like a gunshot to Patrick's heart, making him wince.

"Listen, obviously, I was acting like an ass earlier. I'm sorry, but you have to understand. I can't wait outside for you every day." He quickly glanced at Delan, who said nothing. "Delan, please talk to me. You never got into this much trouble before. I mean, why are you getting detention daily and with Ms. Hawthorne, of all people? She's the nicest teacher I know. How did you manage to piss her off?"

Delan's hand squeezed the assist grip above the door. The crunching of leather beneath his knuckles made Patrick pause. "Delan, what's wrong? Is it your girlfriend?"

"So, what if I have a girlfriend?" he muttered.

"Well, I just want to be there for you."

Delan folded his arms across his chest. "Why would I take help from someone who's never talked to a girl?"

Patrick pulled over to the side of the road and slammed the gears into "Park."

"Look, am I mean to you sometimes? Yes, I am, but that doesn't mean I don't care. If anything is wrong—"

"What's the point of offering help? Like I said, you've never talked to a girl! Not a single one has ever looked your way. Isn't that why you've been doing all that dumb shit to look cool? You know, revving your engine and dressing up as someone completely different! I mean, look how far you've gone!" Delan pulled the handle of the glove compartment, revealing a lighter and grocery list. "I mean, this is pathetic!"

He shoved the note in front of Patrick's face. The note contained only two words, "lighter" and "cigarette."

"This is so stupid. Plus, why smoking? Are you trying to copy those old movies dad has on VHS? No one our age smokes cigarettes and thinks it's cool. Hell, it'd make more sense for you to buy a blunt."

Patrick let his little brother go on his tirade because, no matter how much it made him want to tune him out, Patrick couldn't deny how much his words stung his chest.

"Alright, you can stop now. I'll take you home." Patrick started his car again. This time, he got back on the road the moment he could.

Once they passed a grove of trees and arrived at a traffic light, he looked at his brother once more. With the sunlight painting his face, he looked more innocent than usual. As though they went back when he still had a smile on his face. For the time being, Patrick forced himself to focus on the drive home, choosing to let their argument dissipate into nothing but another distant memory.

As soon as Patrick rolled into the driveway, Delan already clicked on his seatbelt. "Alright then, let's—" before he could finish his sentence, Delan left the vehicle and disappeared into the house. Patrick sat back in his chair in disbelief. *Even my little brother is disappointed in me.* Patrick retrieved his cellphone and began scrolling through his social media apps to pass the time. First, he viewed the pictures of his schoolmates, most of whom never talked to him.

However, he smiled, knowing that the glowing green icon of their profile page showed they followed him. Lily, his old babysitter from years ago, posted frequently. Seeing her enjoying her life after high school brought a smile to Patrick's face. He envied how carefree she was, surrounded by men at her college who seemed to have no problem approaching others.

Suddenly, seeing a young man in one of Lily's pictures hugging her tightly, Patrick frowned. He sighed, knowing that if he were older, he would've asked Lily out on a date. Even if she did outright reject him, at least knowing he tried would be a small confidence booster. After all, he never really saw himself on par with people as social as her.

Let's see. Without hesitation, Patrick searched through more photos of his classmates, both the boys and girls. He tapped on the profile of one of his female peers, but didn't feel much. Even though all the other boys commented on her curvy chest and rear, he couldn't admire her body the same way they did. Instead, he just saw her as a regular person. Neither good nor bad nor attractive.

Different preferences . . .? He tried to reassure himself by using his attraction toward a different girl with less prominent features as justification. Then, reluctantly, he tapped on the photo of a boy in his English class, and unconsciously smiled.

No. He shook his head and told himself to stop acting so strange. *He's just a funny guy.* While Patrick found excitement is ogling at the women around him, the feeling confused him. Almost as though having the same emotions toward both genders felt wrong.

Forget it. Patrick shoved his phone back in his pocket and left the door beside him slightly ajar. The fruity scent of the perfume seeped through the small crack, giving him a moment of reprieve. He figured he had to get rid of all traces of the perfume. But as he was busy airing out his vehicle, a terrifying realization hit him. *The house!* Patrick pushed open the door, intending to burst into his home and opening every window. He couldn't imagine where the perfume lingered.

"I'm surprised you're still outside," his dad said.

Patrick's heart fell at the sound of the man's deep voice. But despite his father's gruff manner of speech, turning around and seeing his face wasn't wholly terrible. "I just wanted to sit in the car for a while."

Without a second thought, his dad said, "I do the same thing. Your mother doesn't understand it, but I need some alone time."

He smiled at him, but quickly gave a look of intrigue.

"Hold on a minute." He stepped beside Patrick and put his face into his car. Patrick's eyes popped wide open when he heard his dad inhale deeply.

"Is that. . . perfume?"

"N-no," Patrick stuttered.

"You have a girlfriend?"

"No."

"Are you lying to me?"

Patrick gave a nervous and quiet chuckle, which garnered a hearty laugh from his dad. "There's no need to be shy."

"Well actually, I. . . I," he stopped speaking and swallowed the lump that developed.

His dad gave Patrick one massive hug. "It's nice that you're finally getting out of your comfort zone. I'm proud of you." He gave Patrick a large pat on the back. The force of his hand jostled his body.

"Thanks."

Patrick felt hesitant to perpetuate the lie, but he knew his mother wouldn't be as happy. After all, she saw her sons as innocent little boys too pure for romance. That's why Patrick felt an immense sense of dread knowing that if Delan didn't hide his neck, they might as well jump into a casket.

"Just remember to let your mother know. Maybe while we're having dinner. I'll cook her favorite meal, so she's in a good mood by then." He winked at Patrick, which eased some of the nervousness away. But as his father entered the house, Patrick stumbled behind him, fighting back the urge to scream into a cooking pot.

September 13th

My Special and Extremely Awesome Journal

I asked Ms. Hawthorne about the high school movies yesterday. She told me she didn't remember most of high school. Said that it was mostly a blur since she hated the place. So I asked her why she became a teacher, and she told me that just because her high school experience was bad, doesn't mean it has to be bad for everyone else. No wonder the other students liked her. Afterward, she let me stay a little longer after the period ended. All we talked about was Patrick. Apparently, she didn't know we were brothers, but what really surprised her was how quiet I was. She told me Patrick was one of her loudest students. Even though he's been keeping to himself lately. I wonder why that is. Maybe he's tired. But what's making him tired? Is it me? We see each a lot at home. Maybe he doesn't want me around? Actually, I think that's a really stupid thought. Oh well, hopefully I can talk to Ms. Hawthorne again. Especially since I hate Mrs. Hart. The woman never stops staring at me. Isn't that weird?

Chapter 3

PAST

Patrick took a moment to calm himself. As he whistled a little tune, his pulse slowed down enough for him to get back into the present moment. He straightened his jacket and entered the house. However, much to his dismay, he found his dad in the process of opening each window.

"I guess the smell got on your brother, and it spread throughout the living room." his dad said as he pulled the glass panes apart forcefully. "Can you turn that on?" He pointed to the ceiling fan.

The moment Patrick flipped the switch, his dad smiled at the spinning blades as though they were a gift from God. "Do you think it'll still be here by the time she gets home?"

"No, but you better be ready to talk to her tonight. I can only do so much to make her happy."

Patrick shrugged his shoulders before adjusting the fan speed. As he dialed the knob, his father watched intently until they silently agreed on the perfect speed. His dad gave him a thumbs up after he set the fan.

The same gesture he displayed in most of their family photos. Each portrait hanging around them showed their entire family in a good light. Even his mom's smile seemed genuine back then, but he couldn't tell if that was only a pose to create the perfect picture.

"Dad, what was Mom like when you first got married?" Patrick asked suddenly.

His dad stuttered before forming a complete sentence. "You're already thinking *marriage*?" he asked sarcastically.

"No, that's not what I meant." Patrick held his gaze, while his dad shrugged his shoulders.

"She was great then, and she still is." He kept his answer short, refusing to elaborate any further. "Anyway, it's about time I start cleaning." Without saying another word, his dad briskly left the living room. The door to his parents' bedroom shut, followed by the sound of a vacuum.

Patrick sighed and opened the fridge. His dad's beer bottles stared back at him like a succubus. Subconsciously, Patrick's hand drifted toward one of them. While his dad let him take the occasional sip, never had they ever given him an entire bottle. Patrick's fingers shook as they wrapped around the glass. In the fridge's light, the beverage called to him.

Isn't that why you've been doing all this dumb shit to look cool? Delan's voice reverberated in his head. Patrick slammed the fridge shut.

"I'm such an idiot." He reluctantly forced himself away from the kitchen. Instead, he mounted the staircase toward his brother's room. The picture frames on the wall felt like a separate entity watching him, telling him how much things have changed. That his life would never be as carefree as it was when he was a child.

"Delan? Patrick said, tapping on his door. He waited for a few seconds before knocking again. "Can I come in?" In response, Patrick heard a pillow thrown at the door. He frowned before giving a warning. "I'm coming in."

"Hey!" his brother yelled.

Patrick put a finger to his lips and shushed him. He quietly closed the door behind them and walked toward his brother. Delan lay on the bed with a tablet next to him. His eyes pierced into Patrick like a knife steadily cutting through butter.

"Listen, Dad smelled that perfume all over me."

Delan paused the video he was watching and sat upright.

"So what? Are you going to tell Mom I have a girlfriend? Is that how you'll get back at me? By making her drill me with nonstop questions all night?"

Patrick shook his head.

"No. Dad assumed it came from me. Plus, I've known Mom's temper a few years longer than you have. So, you should thank me for saving you from all of that." Patrick ran his fingers through his hair, choosing to ignore Delan sticking his tongue out.

"Thanks," his brother muttered, with a hint of animosity.

The tone of his voice made Patrick's blood boil. He missed the days when their bickering only related to the games they played on the playground. Or time they tried to learn Morse code to keep secrets from their parents. "I can tell I'm not the only one bothering you. This 'girl' is still on your mind, isn't she?"

"Can we stop talking about this?" Delan's lips contorted into a pout, resembling the face Patrick saw during his childhood.

He coughed to clear his throat before speaking.

"Fine, but promise me one thing. Talk to someone. Anyone. If something or someone is bothering you, get some help. You don't have to go to me. As long as it's a person you trust."

His little brother eyed him curiously, and when a smile spread across Patrick's face, the boy turned his head away as though ashamed. But Patrick knew he got through to him.

The world fell silent after that, and Delan lowered his head, keeping eye contact with the floor. Soon, his cheeks turned red, making Patrick chuckle internally.

"You always gave me that look before. So, what are you watching?" he asked.

Delan noiselessly tapped the screen of his tablet to let the video play again. "I just wanted to give a brief introduction about myself. Maybe even turn some of my personal experiences into a story you can enjoy." The woman in the video spoke slowly with a soft voice. Her dark black hair and young, round face told Patrick that she wasn't that much older than he was.

"Who's that?" he asked.

"I don't know. Her videos keep getting recommended to me."

Patrick sat beside Delan and laid the tablet on his lap. His brother scooted a little closer as they continued to watch the girl. She said her name was Sofia, and she described her relationship with her mom before diving into her hobby, writing. Patrick took in every little detail, from the tone of her voice to the slow deliberate approach she took when explaining herself.

"I didn't know you enjoyed watching vlog content."

"I like what she has to say," Delan mumbled.

Patrick patted his brother's shoulder.

"Alright then, I'll leave you to it." Delan nodded without taking his eyes off the screen.

"I'm sorry about earlier. You were right. I was acting like a jackass," Patrick said. Delan gave a faint smile and Patrick left his room. Afterward, Patrick dragged his feet across the floor, recognizing slightly more friction from the carpet than usual. His heart fell knowing that his mother would demand he vacuumed the entire upper floor and wipe down the wooden railing even though they were already spotless. And just to add more stress, the events of earlier constantly replayed in his head.

What's going on with me?

He gave the question some more thought, but soon regretted it as he blamed himself. *Am I changing too much? I must be the one bothering him!* Patrick shook his body as though the shame he felt was a mere cloak.

Patrick slumped into his office chair and booted up his computer. With cautious eyes, he briefly glanced over his shoulder, eagerly tapping his fingers on the desk. *Don't walk in. Don't walk in.* The moment every piece of software loaded into place, he doubled clicked the internet browser and typed in the first three letters of his favorite adult site. But as he scrolled through each image, he felt nothing more than pure disappointment. Again, not one pixel of a woman made him smile. Patrick slapped his forehead.

"What the hell is wrong with me?"

He let his mouse cursor hover over a tab that read "Categories." Afterward, he bit hard on his lower lip, fearing that someone would walk in. Before the panic could fully encompass him, he looked up photos and videos of men. All of which made him feel nothing as well. He suppressed the urge to vomit and exited his browser. Afterward, he sat still with his hands covering his face.

No matter what, he found himself stuck in the same cycle. First, he'd look at women and when he felt empty, he'd look at men, and when he felt the same way, he'd try to role play as some psychiatrist digging deep into his brain for an answer.

Repressed sexuality? Distorted sense of self? Homosexuality? Bisexuality? Simple confusion? His pseudo-self-diagnoses changed weekly. He gave a deep grumble before leaning down to grab a can of soda out of the mini fridge next to his desk. And as he lost himself in the sugary high, a message appeared on his screen.

Khen. Messaging Patrick in the app they used for gaming.

Do you still plan on playing a game today?

Patrick examined all the icons of each game installed in his device.

The same one as usual? he texted back, feeling like an idiot for asking. Ever since the school year started, they only played one game together.

Three dots appeared on the screen, letting him know Khen was typing. In the meantime, he started the game and the opening music played through his headset. He went back to the messaging app to turn their texting conversation into a voice call. He double clicked the phone icon, finding himself tapping his nails against the keyboard in perfect rhythm with the ringing.

"So this one again," Khen said through static from his end.

"Are you ready?" Patrick listened to Khen's keyboard clacking through his microphone. In response, Patrick entered his log-in credentials and waited for their session to start.

"Quick question: you know a thing or two about girls, right?" Patrick asked.

"Sure. What do you want to know?"

"Well, Delan walked out of school with perfume all over his clothes and—"

"Wait what? Your little brother pulled a girl before you?" Khen spoke with a loud voice, making a popping sound in his microphone. Patrick flinched as his friend continued to mock him.

"Good job to him."

Patrick sighed. "Just listen to me for a second, okay?"

"Fine."

"Well, since I drove Delan home, the smell spread to my clothes and my dad thought I was the one with a girlfriend. Now, he thinks I am dating someone and expects me to tell my mom. What am I supposed to do?" Patrick spoke feverishly, as though he was ripping away strands of his hair.

"Why not just tell them the truth?"

Patrick shook his head. "I can't. You don't know my mom. Knowing how over-protective she is, she'd start interrogating Delan to make sure he's single. And since he's not. . . well, her tantrums are pretty bad." Patrick leaned forward with his elbows on his desk. "I...I—"

"You're that scared of her?" Khen asked.

"If you lived with her, you'd know. The number of times she's yelled at me for the tiniest things is stupid! Have you ever said something that was taken out of context?"

"Sometimes."

"Imagine living with someone who does that with every little thing. One time, I told my mom that my grades weren't updated and she accused me of lying. Saying that I was a terrible person for hiding my test scores."

"So, my mom does stuff like that." Khen scoffed.

"But your mom doesn't blow up like mine. I'd rather keep up a lie than tell her the truth." Patrick let out a long breath.

"Keeping up a lie is going to be a lot harder."

"I'd rather create a complex story than experience one of her tirades again."

"Alright then, we'll figure something out. The way I see it, you have three options. You could play along with it until the end of time or within a few weeks to a month. You could tell your parents your 'girlfriend' broke things off. And then, there's the best choice. You could get off your ass and find a date." He laughed at his last suggestion, making Patrick tighten his fist over the mouse.

"I'll go with the second option."

"Are you sure? I mean, finding someone would be much better," Khen said with a chuckle.

"I'm sure."

"C'mon. You can find a girl."

Patrick clenched his teeth as he thought back to his browsing history. What if his inability to become attracted to women seeped through? Would everyone make fun of him for it?

"No." A sharp stab hit the back of his head.

"Why? Are you scared?"

"No."

"Gay?"

"Hell, no!" Patrick gritted his teeth and took his anger out by shooting away one of his opponents on the screen. As the player cussed at him, Khen gave out a hearty laugh.

"In that case, I got a great idea. Remember Issac? That genius who graduated early? He's gone to University and been hanging out with all sorts of people. He and some other guys are hosting a bonfire tomorrow night."

Patrick sighed, feeling a sense of disgust in the pit of his stomach. "Listen, I really don't want to go out."

"I'm not taking 'no' for an answer. I'll send him a text and you'll be on your way to the party tomorrow."

Patrick audibly sighed into his microphone.

"Relax, it won't be that bad, alright?"

Patrick jumped out of his chair, letting the end of his headset fight to stay plugged into his computer.

"I said '*NO!*'" he yelled. His shoulders heaved with each breath he took. His chest tightened at the realization that he was on the verge of a panic attack, and he unconsciously dug his fingernails into his desk.

"If you're so nervous about this, you can have a beer when the party starts. All those guys are old enough to buy some. I'm sure they wouldn't mind if we took a bottle or two."

Patrick sat back in his chair. "You never listen to me," he said, defeatedly.

"Well, that's a good thing. Without me, you'd stay inside all day. Plus, I've seen the way you look at your old babysitter when you're scrolling through her photos."

"Khen," Patrick said his name sternly as he pulled his microphone closer to his mouth. He adjusted the microphone, positioning it directly in front of his lips.

"Wouldn't you like to meet someone like her? The girls at that party are around the same age. Have a few drinks and give them a few drinks. It's not like they'll remember anything."

Khen spoke listlessly, with each word seeping out of his mouth like a venomous snake. Patrick's head spun. He realized what his friend was insinuating.

"What's wrong with you?" he asked.

"What do you mean?"

"You know what I mean. Give them a few drinks and they won't remember anything?" He repeated the phrase with slight aggression.

Khen gave a light chuckle as Patrick completely dissociated himself from the video game world. "It's not like anyone will know. You'll be missing out if you don't do this."

Patrick buried his face in his heads. "What am I losing out on? Committing a felony?" Patrick raised his voice once more, but Khen didn't waver in his conviction.

"Like I said, no one will find out. If they remember nothing, how can they tell?"

"If this is what you're planning, I'm not going."

"Oh, hell no. You're going."

Patrick logged out of his game and viewed their messaging app, hovering his mouse cursor over the icon to end the call.

"This is too far."

"You know me. I like dark humor."

"It was never this dark when we were kids," Patrick said quickly.

"Everyone changes a little, don't they?"

"Yeah, I guess so." Patrick listened to Khen clicking away at his mouse before whispering, "*Asshole*," and ending their conversation. He ripped off his headset and paced his room to calm himself before his mom returned.

September 15th

MY JOURNAL

I can't believe I saw Mrs. Hart today at the grocery store. The way she looked at me was just weird. I even scratched the title of this journal to help me forget about it. I don't know what it is about her, but everyone says she gives a lot of attention to her students, almost to the point where everyone feels uncomfortable. A lot of people say it's because she sees us as her own kids, but I already have a mom. Not a nice one, but I'd rather have her than Mrs. Hart. In all honesty, I'm glad I didn't run into her at school today. She's gone and I think everyone's noticed it. The hallways feel a little more open, almost as if we're not being strangled anymore. And best of all, Ms. Hawthorne has us reading 'Romeo and Juliet.' I can't wait for the final assignment. She's already made it clear that we're getting into groups to reenact our favorite scene.

Chapter 4

PRESENT

Patrick stared at his phone screen, listening to Sofia ramble about her life, only to realize how little he knew about his brother. He brought himself back to the day Delan showed him Sofia's content. The way he tuned in to her voice, and proclaimed that he related to her, seemed surreal. What about her did he relate to? Patrick bit down on the nail of his thumb.

"I remember being a kid and seeing the world so drastically different than I do now. Colors weren't the same and I hate to admit it, but some people aren't who they show themselves to be it's an obvious thing to say, which is why I'm upset at how oblivious I was."

Patrick raised his eyebrows, wondering if he was reading too deeply into his brother's mentality when he questioned why his brother sought out this particular content. But then again, his ignorance contributed to the loneliness his brother felt. It would have been better for him to grope hopelessly at the air for an answer rather than remain idle. He brushed away his thoughts.

"That's why I think that town called to me," Sofia said.

Patrick sat upright. Everything about her demeanor changed. Rather than the soft serene environment complimented by her silky hair and light gaze, she grew serious.

Outside, the clouds above rolled in again. They turned gray whilst sending torrents of rain downwards. The gas station parking lot turned into a vast ocean.

"That town, it called to me just as it calls to you."

His phone froze on one frame: Sofia sat quietly on her couch, looking at the camera. A large mirror hung above her, reflecting a woman in a blue dress. One side of the lady's face was scarred black, with orange embers flickering out of the tiny cracks in her skin. But Sofia didn't seem to be fazed, as though the woman wasn't there at all.

Suddenly, despite the frame remaining still, he heard Sofia speak again. This time was nothing more than gibberish. Patrick tossed aside his phone and shook his head.

"What the hell did I just see?" he muttered.

"It'd be best to listen to her," a woman said. Patrick flinched. He brought his eyes to his review mirror, expecting to see someone, but he only saw his brother's clothes beside him in the car. He stepped out of the vehicle. Despite the constant downpour, he stood tall, only to gag at the wretched stench emanating from his trunk. He tightly clasped his hand over his face. With slow, steady strides, he confronted the smell. The rancid odor was something his mother would have snuffed out entirely with every cleaning supply known to man.

Patrick averted his gaze, thinking that it was a mistake to bring Delan's old clothes with him. After all, they were nothing more than memorabilia that needed a good wash. Looking back at the store, he noticed a young man standing behind the register. Without a second thought, Patrick entered the building. As the bright lights attacked his eyes, he heard the employee's faint voice.

"Hi," he said plainly.

Patrick gave him a quick nod.

"Do you sell air fresheners?" he asked, with an awkward smile.

"On the other side of the shelf."

"Thanks." Patrick rounded the corner. He scoured the labels of each product. After some time, he rested his fingers on a spray bottle, but when he sprayed it he gagged almost as horribly as he had at the scent marinating inside his trunk. The bottle exuded a fruity smell as strong as perfume. He aggressively sorted through each item, hoping to find something different. *Strawberry. Lemon. Cherry.* The labels stirred a deep sensation of resentment in him.

"Do you have anything that's just 'odorless?'" he asked, returning to the cashier.

The man shrugged his shoulders. "Nope, sorry. All the ones we sell are made from smells to mask the bad ones."

Patrick sighed, but quickly apologized.

"It's okay. You can't help it."

"No need to say 'sorry.' I get it. Sometimes you don't want other people's scents lingering around you. It sounds petty, but the reason I took this job was to get out of my dorm. The girls across the hall spray perfume everywhere."

"Dorm?"

The man nodded.

"Yes. You'd be surprised by people's actions. Some try to be high and mighty; some spray themselves with almost anything like a middle schooler worshipping Axe body spray, and some are just like me, trying to pass by."

"You're in school then?"

"Yes, Iowa State University."

"Iowa? You've traveled quite far then." Patrick narrowed his eyes on him, wondering why someone from the Midwest came all the way to Alaska just to work at some gas station.

The man looked at him perplexedly.

"No, not really." He shook his head, and Patrick figured it was pointless.

Summer job in Alaska? He wanted to ask the young man.

"What's your name?"

The cashier ran a finger across his nametag.

"I'm Luke."

While Patrick tried to come up with what to say next, Luke simply sat back in his chair and pulled a sketchbook out. "Is there anything else you need?"

"No, nothing." Patrick turned around to observe the cleaning supplies once more. He occasionally glanced over his shoulder to see Luke running a pencil across a page in his book.

"Is that my car?" Patrick asked quickly, turning around. He pointed at a detailed sketch of his vehicle on the white paper. "Have you been watching me?"

"No. I just saw your car outside and tried to recreate it from memory. It's for my class. I want to be a forensic sketch artist."

Patrick tilted his head to the side, wondering how someone could talk so confidently.

"When were you staring at my car?"

"I wasn't ogling at it for long. Like I said, I drew from memory." Luke set down his pencil, putting his hands to rest beside the register.

"That doesn't answer my question. *When* did you look at my car?" Patrick did his best to stand taller.

"A few minutes ago."

"Then you must have seen someone else out here too, right? I heard a woman talking to me!"

"I didn't see anyone else."

Patrick observed Luke pulling his sketchbook closer to him, as if he was hiding something. His actions stirred a sense of paranoia. Patrick snatched Luke's work. With the student stared in disbelief, Patrick flipped through the pages. Each drawing was the face of a different person, extremely detailed. "Have you been watching these people?"

Calmly, Luke took the book as Patrick's grip loosened.

"No, like I said, I recreate everything from memory. Plus, it gets boring out here. Barely anyone talks to me."

Patrick shook his head.

"Okay, sure." He spoke cautiously.

"By the way, thank you for paying."

"What?"

"The money. I saw the money laid out on the counter. Most people run off with something. Hell, I'd say you're probably one of the nicest people I've come across while working here."

Patrick quietly nodded his head as he lost himself in his own confusion. From the brief but memorable events that took place in his vehicle to the strange talents Luke displayed, everything about today was unexpected.

"If I'm the nicest, you must get a lot of rude customers. After all, I bet no one has yelled at you and snatched your sketchbook."

Luke nodded.

"That's true, but you're right to be weirded out. Having your car drawn like this seems like something a stalker would do. What brings you here, anyway?" Luke let out a wide smile, showing off his teeth. His face made Patrick grimace.

"My brother and I came here once."

"Is the gas station really that important to you?"

Patrick grinned.

"No, but Alaska is. It was only one trip, but we never forgot it."

Luke furrowed his eyebrows.

"Right, Alaska..." Luke retrieved a canned coffee from under the counter and pushed it over toward Patrick. "There's no need to pay for it. Just drink it to wake up. Seems like you need it more than anyone else."

Patrick quietly consumed the drink as he stared out the window. Meanwhile, Luke watched him intently, like an eagle eyeing its prey. Ripples of water from the rain washed mud down the hill by the road, creating a small barricade of dirt.

Patrick thought back to his childhood. Of how much Delan hated rain because without the perfect weather, their mother would keep them inside as though the droplets of wind or snow were poison to their skin. A quick flash of lightning showed itself in the distance, followed by the ringing of the bell that hung above the door.

"Welcome in," Luke said, instinctively. Both of them brought their attention to the doorway, where Charlie stood, wagging his tail. "That damn mutt." Luke's face twisted into a frown as Charlie bared his teeth. Patrick darted his eyes between the two, expecting them to get into a brawl.

"You know him?" Patrick asked, approaching Charlie.

"Not really, but he stops by now and then. He always greets the customers. Even the bad ones."

"Well, it sounded like you knew him." Patrick patted Charlie, who was still on his hind legs, ready to leap forward. "I bet he knows you."

While Luke put a finger to his chin, humming deeply, the surrounding air moved swiftly out the door as if the wind was being sucked right out of the building. Only when the odd sensation pass did Patrick find himself back at the counter, where Luke was flipping through his sketchbook. Patrick looked down and saw the can of coffee he had just finished was still sealed.

"What the heck?" he muttered.

Luke looked up from the pages.

"Is everything okay?" he asked in a friendlier tone.

Patrick tightly squeezed the can. His hands trembled as he tried to reassess the situation. *Wasn't I at the open door? Didn't I step outside? Why am I back here?*

"Where's Charlie?" he asked, confused.

"Who?"

"The dog." Patrick looked to the door that remained vacant.

"Oh yeah," Luke said with astonishment. "I've met some really messed-up people here. I'm surprised none of them tried to kill me," he said, quickly.

"Hold on. Don't change the subject. Where's Charlie?"

"Who?"

"Charlie. I was standing at the door earlier, don't you remember?" The feeling of the air being sucked out of the building returned. Patrick's vision contorted into one big blur while the hairs on his arm were being pulled by some unknown force. Only then did he stand at the door again, in front of Charlie. Patrick peered down at the dog's face, who appeared unfazed, as though they were both always standing there.

Am I getting lost in my head again?

Luke nodded. "Yup. The last person to come through was a woman. Like you, she was one of the few people who took the time to talk to me. She confessed to me about screwing over her husband in a divorce settlement. That dog followed her everywhere." Again, Luke spoke on and on without acknowledging Patrick's questions.

And much to his frustration, Patrick had little hope that he could get through to him and explain the odd phenomenon.

"Do you think she owned him?" Patrick asked, playing with the conversation. He watched Luke intently to see if he could get his demeanor to shift.

"No, I think the mutt just enjoys being around people, no matter who they are. I never saw that woman again, though."

Patrick gave up on expressing the sudden shift he experienced and just petted Charlie. He held his hand out, and the canine sniffed it before jumping forward. Patrick caught him in a half-hearted hug. But when he felt a powerful tug on his shirt sleeve, he realized Charlie had sunk his teeth into it. He ripped it off before standing still as though nothing had happened.

"You, okay?" Luke asked, rushing over.

"Yes, he didn't bite me. Just my clothes."

"Get out!" Luke yelled at Charlie.

"Hold on. I don't think he meant it. He's just being playful."

Luke raised his eyebrows. "You sure? If that thing mauls you and my boss finds out, he'll fire me for not getting rid of that dog."

Despite Luke's words, Charlie only smiled and his tongue hung out of his mouth.

"Yeah, I'm sure," Patrick said. Then, without warning, Charlie sprinted out of the store and stood behind Patrick's car.

"What the hell do you have back there? Dog treats?" Luke pointed at Patrick's trunk.

"No. Just some clothes."

"The damn dog must be hungry for another shirt."

Patrick shrugged his shoulders. He fumbled with the end of his battered shirt sleeve.

"I'll go see what he wants."

"You're a strange guy, you know that?" Luke asked as Patrick stepped out the door. While the young man waited behind his register, Patrick met Charlie at the trunk of his car.

"I know it smells bad, but I promise to clean it." He spoke to the friendly husky in a soft tone, a mere whimper. Together, they stood silently, viewing the back of the car.

"Wait!" Patrick gripped Charlie by the collar as the dog bit hard into a sliver of a red sleeve sticking out. At the touch of Patrick's hand, Charlie transformed into a growling beast. He sunk his teeth deep into the fabric, refusing to let go.

"Stop!" Patrick screamed, pushing aside his confusion from earlier to ensure he preserved his brother's clothes. But when he tugged on Charlie's collar, he fell backward.

The dog's four legs towered over Patrick as he lay on the pavement. While rain splattering on his face, he wondered if he finally looked as battered on the outside as he had felt these past four years on the inside. He eyed the fabric sticking out before waving a finger in front of Charlie.

"That belongs to Delan," he said harshly. But after Charlie whimpered, Patrick's face took on a softer appearance. "Go." He directed the animal toward the side of the car, opening the passenger side door. Patrick moved the bundle of Delan's clothing to the backseat. After a moment's hesitation, Charlie hopped inside, patiently waiting for Patrick to join him. And once they both cozied themselves within the vehicle, they sat motionless. Rather than shaking off his heavy coat, Charlie stared out at the water below the cliff.

"Delan, loved dogs, you know?" Patrick gave a wry smile while Charlie gave a quiet whimper. "I'm sorry." Patrick scooted closer and let his fingers dance through Charlie's soaked fur. Layers of liquid drenched his hand. "Feel free to shake off and dry yourself. I won't get mad, I promise."

At his permission, Charlie wiggled his entire body, sending a flurry of water shooting against the glass. Meanwhile, Patrick sat back, trying to figure out which splotches came from the storm and which ones came from the dog.

What? A pair of quivering, feminine lips flashed in his rear-view mirror. The moment he turned around, they disappeared. Only his little brother's clothes looked back at him. Patrick squinted his eyes, not knowing what he just saw.

"Welcome! Welcome!" said a voice on the radio. Voices of dozens of talk show hosts filled his ears. While the dial remained stationary, the names of each podcast lit up the dashboard like Christmas light, until it finally settled on an unknown frequency. The number read "303."

"I had experienced familial problems in the past," Sofia's voice spoke. "But now, I see I put the blame on the wrong person. For all of you who follow me, do you feel the same way? Have you ever gotten so mad at someone who doesn't deserve it?"

Patrick slapped the radio, sending a whirl of static his way. Charlie barked at it.

"Guilt. Justice. Vengeance." A different woman's voice spoke. This time, it sounded older, more mature. "What actions have you taken?" What have you done?"

Patrick covered his ears as hundreds of voices spoke through the speakers in unison. "What have you done?" Patrick let out a booming screech, only to flinch at the tiny pieces of debris flying forward. Charlie sunk his teeth into the radio, shutting everything off. Despite knowing he'd have to pay for damages, Patrick pulled Charlie in for a hug. "Thank you," he said.

September 16th

MY JOURNAL

Bad news. Turns out Mrs. Hart is back. For the first time, I skipped class, specifically her class. But of course, I get caught. Ms. Hawthorne ran into me the moment I went into the courtyard. Luckily, she wasn't mad. Although she told me to never skip my classes again. Oh well, at least I ran into her instead of the faculty members. If only more teachers could be like her. I really hate everyone else here and worse of all, I'm hating Patrick a little more, too. He's changed. He's not the same person I remember. What happened to spending the afternoon together, sitting on the couch playing games? Now he's spending at least an hour after school ends revving his engine in the parking. I even caught him trying to buy cigarettes. Thankfully, the cashier called him out for being a minor. Still, I hate how much things have changed.

Chapter 5

PAST

Patrick and Delan sat beside each other at the dinner table. Patrick gave his brother a nervous glance, hoping to see the boy acknowledge him, but when Delan stared straight ahead except to sip at his glass, the tension in Patrick's chest grew more intense. While plates of food and cups dotted the white tablecloth, their mother's stern look infected the pristine display. The way her brown eyes pierced into the dishes made Patrick's stomach queasy. Her silent display of anger was like watching rain clouds form before a massive storm. He eyed his father, who quietly chewed his own food.

"What did you guys do for school?" their mom asked. Delan lowered his head and nudged Patrick with his knee. *You seriously want me to go first?*

"I took a test. Don't know what my score is yet, but I think I passed." Patrick took a gulp of water from his glass.

"You think?" His mother rested her elbows on the table and leaned forward. Patrick nervously nodded. "Why can't you be sure?" While her breath came out in a low hum, Patrick's eye twitched.

He already knew his answer, but the words tangled in his throat, knowing that they weren't the words she wanted to hear.

"Because they haven't graded it." Patrick kept his eyes on his plate and anxiously ground the tip of his fork into the platter. The sound emanated throughout the room, making Delan quiver.

"And when will your grade come out?" she asked sternly.

"I don't know."

"I already told you to stop saying that," she snapped at him.

"I'm sorry," Patrick whispered. He gently pushed against the table, slowly making distance between himself and the white tablecloth.

"How many times do I have to tell you? Answer me properly."

"Okay, I will." Patrick let out a deep breath, but it didn't relax him.

"There you go again," she scolded. "Stop saying 'okay.' I want you to answer me properly."

Patrick's heart sent a shockwave pulsating through his body.

How do you want me to answer you? he thought to himself.

Seeing as how his mother's mood was already reaching a breaking point, Patrick stayed silent. He took a few more bites of the dinner his dad had prepared them, hoping that his mother would drop the conversation.

"Well, will you answer me?"

Patrick gulped hard while Delan's eyes grew wide.

"I'm sorry, but my teacher didn't tell me when she will post the grades." His voice wavered, which garnered a nasty look from his mom.

"You don't have to speak so formally to me. You're my son." She gritted her teeth, making her last words come out as more of a hiss.

"Okay." As soon as the words left his lips, Patrick bit down on the inside of his cheek. His mom slapped her hands on the table and leaned forward. Patrick turned his head away slightly to avoid meeting her eyes.

"It's okay. We can check his grades later," his dad said calmy. At his father's interjection, his mother sat back down, taking up her own glass. Seeing her chugging down her water like nothing happened put Patrick on edge, leaving him to wonder what would set her off next. Meanwhile, Delan pretended to be oblivious. He looked at the ceiling the same way he did when he was a kid.

"Hey, chew quietly!" their mother barked at Delan.

"It's okay," their dad said.

Patrick took in a deep breath, thankful to have his dad by their side. He just wished his mother was still the patient saint he remembered her to be when he was a very young child.

"Anyway, Patrick, don't you have something to share?" His dad gave a tight smile.

From there, Patrick felt sweat form around his temples. *Of course, the fake girlfriend.* He knew his father would bring it up eventually. Yet, it still felt surreal hearing him allude to it, especially in the volatile state his mother was in. He waited for a few seconds to steel his nerves.

"Patrick?" his father said again.

"Y-yes, that's right." His voice grew fainter with each word. His hand trembled against his silverware as he brought the spoonful of pork up to his mouth. Meanwhile, Delan remained invisible.

"What do you have to say?" his mom asked. In response, he stuttered, forcing her to snap her fingers. "What is it?" Her tone turned even more aggressive. Patrick watched the blade of her knife chop down through her portion of pork, eviscerating the meat the same way anxiety was eviscerating his body. "You know, if by eventful, your father means you got into some trouble, then I'm not having any of that." Her eyelid twitched as she stared at him. Everyone else at the table slightly dipped their heads, looking toward the plates.

"I have a girlfriend," Patrick whispered too softly for anyone to hear.

His mother raised an eyebrow.

"Why are you speaking so quietly?" she asked in a soft voice. Her smooth hand rested on top of his, making his heart stop. He knew what her actions meant. Every time he had difficulty speaking, she'd touch him gently, as though her skin was a snake whispering sweet nothings into his ear. But no matter how much she manipulated him, the gentle touch never failed to make him lower his guard. So, he spoke, knowing an icy rage would burst out soon.

"I-I'm sorry."

"Patrick, it's okay. You can use your voice." She fluttered her eyelashes like a doll. "Patrick." At the sound of her voice cracking, Patrick suppressed the urge to gasp. Delan's pupils dilated as he tapped his finger against the wooden table.

"Tell me, what's so eventful about Patrick's school days?" she asked their father. The man, once lively, resembled a statue.

He kept his head held high, but the youthful light extinguished from his hollow eyes. "Patrick, I think you should share the good news."

"Well, out with it." A miniscule sliver of spit escaped his mother's lips.

"I have a girlfriend." The lie came out just as quickly as his mom's hardened glare.

Delan's eyes grew wide. Patrick nudged him in the ribs, causing his body to jerk slightly while he mouthed the words "you owe me."

"Girlfriend?"

"Yes, mom. I have a girlfriend."

His mother put down her fork and began pouring herself another glass of water. Right before she completely drained the pitcher, her hand tilted upward, slowly decreasing the speed of the waterfall she created. Patrick's eyes locked onto the liquid, imagining it as sand in an hourglass, and once her cup was full, she grumbled.

"What's her name?" she asked with a slight venom to her words.

Patrick thought for a moment to come up with something. His mind raced back to the video Delan had played him earlier. "Sofia," he blurted.

His mom hummed her lips. "And is she a nice girl?"

"Yes."

"Are you sure?"

"Yes."

"And you can still keep up with your schooling?"

"Yes."

Finally, their mother slammed her glass down on the table. A crack rippled through it, letting a few droplets of water seep through.

"Answer me properly!" she yelled. Everyone at the table jumped in their seats. "Stop giving me short answers," his mother grunted before returning to her food. "You better start acting your age. Otherwise, you'll never leave this house."

Patrick quietly nodded. He lowered his head, noticing Delan's somber face next to him.

"Done," Delan said, standing with his empty plate. He raced back to his bedroom, forcing their mother to sigh.

"I don't get that boy. He is always keeping to himself."

Patrick pursed his lips and looked to his dad, who was already slipping into a food induced coma. "Thank you," he said. Just like Delan, his dad quickly left the dining room. Patrick sat in silence, listening to his mother chew while anticipating another outburst. His phone vibrated in his pocket, and he took a quick peek beneath the tablecloth.

Thank you, his brother texted him. Patrick turned off his device and tried to finish his food. He got up and left with his plate still half full. At the top of the staircase, he looked over his shoulder only to see his mother staring at the wall, appearing lost in her own head.

"Delan," Patrick whispered while tapping on his door.

"Come in."

Immediately, Patrick entered and shut them inside for privacy.

"Listen, you owe me one. I swear mom will come after me again."

"I know," Delan said sadly. He remained on his bed and rolled onto his back while holding his phone. Sofia's voice spoke in the background as she discussed her own relationship with her mother. While the girl spoke calmly and deliberately, her words struck deep into Patrick's chest. However, rather than relating to her, the pain within him stemmed from the fact that he and Sofia were completely different. While she stated that she should have loved her mom for being such a noble woman, Patrick only wished he could say the same for his.

"The least you can do is get out of school on time. At least then, I won't be so stressed out wondering where you are."

Delan paused the video, turned to his side, and faced his brother to answer him.

"I will, I promise."

Patrick gave a faint smile, feeling satisfied with his brother's words. The boy's enunciation, complemented by his blunt response, was enough evidence for Patrick to know he was telling the truth.

"You've changed a lot, but promise me it's for the better," Patrick said. With that, he left his brother's bedroom and returned to his own.

After shutting himself inside his abode, Patrick sat at his desk with his head down. He breathed a sigh of relief and rested his finger on the power button of his monitor. The sight of his face reflected in the screen's blackness erupted a surge of anger. Patrick tapped his fingers across the keyboard, knowing full well that his immediate future seemed rather bleak. What if his lies came crashing down?

September 17th

MY JOURNAL

I'd like to say that today was a good day, but I can't. Sometimes, Patrick is too much for me. I know that sounds awful to say, but I hate seeing him like this. Again, he spent another hour revving his car in the parking lot. He even begged one of the college students in town to buy him a pack of cigarettes. I've never seen him like this. Why can't he see how stupid he looks? I tried to ask him to play a game today. The same one we played when we were kids, but when I got to his door, I didn't even bother to knock. I hear him and Khen talking on the computer again. And to be honest, it made me wish I was deaf. Khen's is just a massive pervert, and so is Patrick. Can't they talk about something else? Don't they get bored ogling over girls over and over again? I'm planning to talk to Patrick about this, but I've never confronted him before. After all, I was the one following him all the time. But it's just been so unbearable watching him trying out all these new things and forgetting about me.

Chapter 6

PAST

Patrick didn't have to sulk too long before Khen messaged him again, begging to start another gaming session. Patrick obliged, although once they started playing, he found himself ready to pull his hair out. His friend bombarded their teammates with cusses and insults as they found themselves on the losing end of the battle.

"Patrick!" Khen's voice cracked, loud in Patrick's ears in the headphone world of the video game.

"Alright. I get it." Patrick obeyed his friend's commands half-heartedly. While the game offered a form of escape, he was learning to associate each session with hatred the moment Khen took part.

"What the hell are you doing?" A loud slam followed by many keystrokes echoed from Khen's line.

Patrick let out a scoff and stood from his chair.

"I'm going to bed," he said. He spoke quickly and logged out of the game before he could hear more verbal abuse. Afterward, he paced his room. By now, the darkness of the night had set in and the digital clock on Patrick's wall reminded him how little sleep he'd get. He rested his hand against the wall and leaned on it. He slowly raised each finger as he counted how many hours of sleep he could indulge in before 7:00 am. His heart broke apart when he only raised five fingers.

Damn it! Patrick flipped his light switch off, making his mattress appear as nothing more than a giant marshmallow. He put one foot in front of the other. Suddenly, a blinding white beam flew across his window. He raised his hand to cover his eyes. Through the tiny slits in his blinds, he realized it was only the headlights from a vehicle was driving by. He let out a deep breath, figuring that it must have been the neighbors, but when it stopped on the curb beside his house, he froze. *Who the hell is that?*

Patrick scooted himself to the edge of the pane, making sure to only stick one side of his head into view. While he couldn't distinguish the figure inside, he saw the slender outline of someone sitting behind the steering wheel. Suddenly, his room turned pitch black as the driver turned off their headlights. Patrick reached for his phone to use as a flashlight, but by the time he brought the device to the window, the car was already gone. He slapped himself on the forehead.

"It's just someone who has a better social life than me," he muttered. Patrick sank into his bed, trying to tell himself the woman was just someone who returned from a night spent bar hopping and got confused. Or it could have been some man going out on a date or some late-night rendezvous. Either way, each made up scenario helped rest Patrick's shaking palms.

He shut his eyes and listened to the howling winds to put himself to sleep. A warm smile spread over his face and he brought the sheets up to his chin. As his breath steadied for sleep, he was interrupted by the sound of Delan, sobbing.

Patrick shot upward, threw his legs over the mattress, and marched out of his room. His toe smashed against the corner of his doorway.

"Delan!" he called out. In the dark, Patrick stumbled toward the light emanating from the bathroom. "Delan!" He yanked open the door, revealing his brother sitting on the floor beside the toilet, crying profusely.

"Don't look at me!" Delan muttered through chattering teeth.

Patrick flinched and raised his hands.

"What's going on? You feel sick?"

When his brother didn't respond, Patrick took a step forward.

"Stop." Delan glared at him with an expression of anger and fear. His long stare and glazed eyes made him appear distant, as though he came from another realm.

Patrick rested on the ball of his foot as he stayed rooted in place. He captured every inch of Delan to ensure he wasn't missing any small but important details.

"Okay, I'll stay right here, but please, tell me what's going on."

His brother sniffled to himself as his hand trembled inside his coat. *Coat?* he thought, realizing his brother was dressed as though he had left the house. His favorite sneakers and leather jacket were still on him, and he'd combed his hair slightly.

"Had a bad night out?" Patrick asked, but his question only garnered a larger sob than before. His sibling's reaction forced him to stand still. Once again, the familiar scent of fruity perfume filled his nostrils. This time, Patrick sensed coconut rather than strawberries.

"Delan, please tell me what's going on." Patrick took a gentle step forward, immediately causing his brother to turn ballistic.

"I told you to leave me alone!" he yelled. Both of them fell silent. The sound of their father's snores echoed through the house while the pattering of an unknown liquid slowly became more apparent.

Through it all, Patrick tuned into the sound, realizing that it came from Delan. Initially, he assumed perhaps he had gotten so frightened he urinated, but upon closer inspection, he noticed that the liquid was red. It seeped out from under his brother's jacket.

"Delan I..."

Before he could finish, his brother opened his coat, showing the knife he gripped by the blade. The serrated edges dug into his skin, but he showed no hints of physical pain. Instead, his torment seemed to focus more on some unknown fear.

"What can I do for you?" Patrick asked nervously.

But his brother only rested his forehead against the toilet seat.

"You can just leave me alone."

"I'm sorry, but I can't do that." He extended his hand. "Let me help you."

Delan turned his head away as more tears flowed out.

"You can't. You can't help me. Things can't go back to the way they were. Not after tonight."

Patrick gulped. "What do you mean? What happened?"

"It doesn't matter. Nothing matters!"

As Delan slowly raised the blade, Patrick ran forward.

"Stop!"

The bathroom walls swallowed his voice, keeping it contained from the rest of the house. "Delan, hand over the knife." Patrick slowed his pace with his arms outstretched.

But rather than hearing him out, Delan kicked Patrick's knee, knocking him down. Patrick grunted and by the time he sat upright, Delan was already holding the knife to his throat. "If you move, I'll kill myself right here!"

Patrick's pupils dilated at his brother's threats. He couldn't fathom what may have happened to the little boy he once knew, or what happened during the night while he was at his computer. After all, once dinner ended, his brother stayed inside watching videos on his tablet.

"Dad!" Patrick yelled, sticking his head out of the bathroom. After he called for his father, he lunged forward, seeing that Delan was ready to drive the blade into his throat. They wrestled against the wall.

"Sorry for this," he whispered. As children, they'd get into the occasional fight, and in every single altercation, Patrick managed to win. But with a knife in play, he didn't know if he could reach the same result. "Stop struggling!"

He mounted Delan, attempting to grab the knife handle. But Delan pushed back, slightly nicking Patrick's wrist with the tip of the blade.

"Dad!" Patrick yelled again. This time, as his voice grew harsher, a rumbling from downstairs became clear.

He heard heavy footsteps striding through the living room.

"Dad! Delan is trying to kill himself!" he screamed. At his announcement, he heard his father's heavy steps turning into a sprint.

"What did you do?" Delan asked in a sad voice.

In his brother's moment of faltering, Patrick punched him in the face. From there, the knife flew across the bathroom floor, and the moment Delan crawled toward the weapon, Patrick pulled him into a tight hug.

"Please, don't hurt yourself," he whispered. "I'll be here. I always will."

"What the hell is going on?" their dad asked from the doorway.

While Delan cried into Patrick's chest, Patrick looked up at his father. Without speaking, they both nodded their heads. Once his dad picked up the knife, he mouthed the words "stay with him," as he left the bathroom. Soon afterward, he heard his dad on the phone speaking to a 911 operator.

Meanwhile, he didn't hear a peep out of his mother. He assumed that he'd have a lot of explaining to do when the ambulance arrived and woke her up.

December 13th

MY JOURNAL

It's been so long since I've held this journal. It's been so long since I've done almost anything. I can't help but walk through the hallways with headphones over my ears. Most of the time, I imagine an 'x' over everyone's faces to remind me I don't exist to them. It's a shame. These are the people Patrick wants to impress. He's ignoring me so he can fit in with these guys. Are they really that important to him? So important that he ditch me just so he can play as some tough guy in the parking lot? It's so stupid. If it wasn't for Ms. Hawthorne, I'd probably have given up on everything, including this journal, but I guess English teachers have a knack for getting students to read and write. It's too bad she won't let me stay in her classroom for long. It's not like I have anywhere else to be.

Chapter 7

PRESENT

Patrick watched each raindrop on his windshield as he ran his fingers through Charlie's fur. Occasionally, the dog would growl, and Patrick couldn't fathom why. Initially, he thought the animal noticed someone in the distance, but each time Patrick scanned their surroundings, he saw nothing but rain. Again, another low grumble reverberated through Charlie's throat. Patrick shushed him.

"It's okay," he said. But despite his reassurance, Charlie continued to stare through the windshield at something that wasn't there. Patrick grimaced at the dog, feeling annoyed.

What's gotten into you? he thought, squinting his eyes at the railing. The rain, combined with the mildew of the early morning, changed the scenery. The once slightly fogged-over view of the lake had changed to a vast field of gray fog, shrouding the large body of water entirely. Charlie twisted his head to the side, staring at the gas station. A deep growl escaped his throat. Patrick squinted his eyes and followed his gaze.

In the distance, beside the building, were three men. All appeared to be about Patrick's height, and while it was impossible to discern any specific facial features, they looked shockingly alike. Albeit, two of them appeared ragged, as though the world had torn them down, while one appeared more stoic and contained, with a freshly lit cigarette resting between his lips.

Patrick rapidly blinked his eyes, unable to believe his own vision. A few blinks later, Patrick saw the men disappear, and a great weight lifted from his chest.

I'm losing my damn mind.

Charlie barked at the area where the men had just been standing, sending a shockwave of fear shooting through Patrick's body. *It can't be. I must be seeing things.* He popped open his car door and stepped outside in the rain.

"It's just us, okay? This damn parking lot is empty!" He spoke confidently, refusing to believe what he saw. "If people were out there, I'd see them right now."

Not earlier. But now.

Again, Charlie barked at him. Patrick shook his head and scoffed. He turned his attention toward the trunk, which was reeking even more.

"Stay," he commanded. He headed toward the gas station, deciding it'd be best to mask the smell until he reached Skagway.

"Welcome back," Luke said without taking his eyes off his sketchbook.

"Hi." Patrick grabbed a pile of cleaning supplies from the shelf and dropped them on the front counter. His previous interaction with Luke replayed constantly in his head, but Patrick brushed it aside and gave in to the idea that he was simply losing his sense of reality because of exhaustion.

Luke eyed the products and furrowed his brows in confusion.

"Are you really planning on cleaning your car now?" He turned his head to the window, where they both took in the heavy rain.

"I just want to hide the smell from my brother's clothes."

Luke smirked at him.

"Your brother's clothes? Did he really leave you with his dirty laundry?"

Patrick sighed and gave him a nasty look.

"Just let me buy the damn items."

Luke shrugged his shoulders.

"Okay then. Oh, by the way, I looked into that girl you told me about, Sofia. Her videos are relatively new, and I can't tell if she's making things up."

"What do you mean?"

"Well, in her recent video, she's talking about some weird town along with feelings of guilt and punishment. It's like she's crazy or trying to create some sort of narrative with these videos."

Patrick raised an eyebrow.

"What are you talking about?"

"In her last video she kept saying—"

"Kept saying what?" Patrick leaned closer to listen to Luke, but still couldn't make out what he was saying.

"It's the name of a town, but I've never heard of it."

"Okay, but which town?"

"I just said it was '—'." Again, the name didn't register in Patrick's brain as though Luke was purposefully going silent.

"Look, I'm not in the mood for this. My car smells like shit, and I want to clean it up. So, sell me the products or finish your sentences."

"Okay. I guess you're not interested in her story then," Luke said sarcastically. "But '—' is such a weird name for a town."

Patrick clenched his teeth. He slapped his hand on the counter and reached into his pocket.

"Just ring everything up."

Luke flinched as Patrick's strike created a massive boom in their tiny building.

"Alright, but lighten up a bit."

"Fine." Despite the frustration, Patrick couldn't deny that he still felt a sense of remorse for treating Luke the way he did. In his eyes, the guy was probably just bored sitting inside.

"Here." Once Luke finished scanning every item, he handed them over while Patrick kept his card in the card reader.

"Listen, I'm sorry for being a little tired," Patrick said. While his words weren't completely true, at the very least, he hoped it would lessen the impact of his rudeness.

"Take it." Luke reached underneath the counter and slid over a can of coffee.

"Another one? How much is it?"

"Don't worry about paying for it. It's on me."

Patrick twiddled his fingers inside his wallet. He and Luke made eye contact, before Patrick shrugged his shoulders and said, "Thanks." He opened the can and pressed it against his lips, savoring the taste. "I can't imagine what Sofia must be thinking of."

Luke pursed his lips. "Her family situation sounds real, but definitely not the paranormal aspect."

"She said she was writing a book. You think she's just talking about her life and how it inspires her story?"

Luke obviously considered what Patrick said, but ultimately didn't seem to come up with a concrete answer.

"I'm not sure. I only started watching her content after you mentioned it. Anyway, watch her latest upload. The way she talks about guilt and punishment is so creepy."

At his words, a crack of thunder echoed in the distance. Patrick bowed his head slightly to take another sip.

Guilt? He thought about the word for a while before dismissing himself from the conversation.

"Thank you," he said, leaving the store with his bag of supplies. As he approached his vehicle, he found Charlie sleeping soundly in the passenger's seat while Delan's clothes were in disarray. The ugly sight of his brother's tarnished clothing made him crush the can. His fingers punctured a hole in it as he took a deep breath.

Dogs will act like dogs. He looked at Charlie, knowing that he should have expected the animal to shed its fur on everything. But for the time being, he ignored him and walk around to the trunk. However, once he came face to face with the rear of his car, he stopped, noticing a blue piece of fabric.

"What the hell?" he muttered. The clouds above grew darker, making him feel a bit more uneasy. The blue strip rested on top of the rear lights. He took it and examined it. After running his fingers across the fabric, he concluded it must have come from something made with a lot of care and precision. Perhaps a fancy dress. Certainly nothing Delan would have worn.

Upon further inspection, he realized that the red on his taillight wasn't from the bulb itself, but from blood.

Patrick touched it, and a crimson line stuck to his fingertips.

Fresh?

"Charlie!" Patrick ran toward the passenger's side and pulled open the door. The dog barked loudly and jumped against the concrete. "We need to go!"

Patrick beckoned for him to follow, fearing that whoever left those markings was still lingering around. He wanted to run back inside the gas station and yell at Luke to lock the door, but Charlie ran toward the trunk. Patrick pursued him, fearing for the animal's safety.

"What the hell?"

His trunk had changed once again.

This time, a white sleeve stuck out from the tightly shut compartment. Charlie growled before biting into it. He tugged, trying to rip it off.

"Stop!" Patrick yelled at him. He stomped both feet into the ground to get a better bearing while he pulled Charlie by the torso. As their struggle turned into a game of tug of war, Charlie growled louder until, eventually, the sleeve tore off completely. Together, they fell backward, with Patrick taking the largest brunt of the force.

"We need to go. We need to go now!" Patrick rolled over onto his stomach, fighting against the pain in his head as he forced himself to stand. He gripped Charlie's collar and stumbled toward the station.

"Charlie...hurry."

The next thing Patrick saw was a small drop of blood falling from his chin to the ground. When he pressed his fingers against his scalp, he realized the pavement had left a large cut. Blood seeped through and drenched his fingers.

He lay down on his side as the dizziness took hold of him.

"Charlie," Patrick whispered. But the dog looked past him, growling at someone nearby. "Who is it? Who's there?"

Patrick's eyes watched helplessly as Charlie ignored him. In one quick motion, the canine opened his mouth wide and leaped over Patrick. He heard him chasing someone into the distance. Soon, the sounds of his barking faded, leaving only the heavy patter of rain. With his clothes soaked, Patrick shut his eyes, praying that Luke would take notice of his broken body and come to his rescue.

December 15th

MY JOURNAL

It sounds stupid, but I put myself in detention. Today, I insulted Ms. Hawthorne during class. Everyone stared at me, wondering how I could do such a thing, and while I felt awful, I just want to talk to her. Everyone says she's the nicest teacher and I can see why. I plan to come clean and tell her I just wanted to get detention, so I wouldn't feel lonely. Hopefully, she'll know that I didn't mean what I said, but even then, I never thought I'd be able to come up with such horrible things to say.

Chapter 8

PAST

Patrick lost track of time as Delan remained in a perpetual state of shock. The young man hadn't utter a single word since Patrick disarmed him. Instead, he reverted to a younger state. He made nonsensical noises while gripping onto Patrick's arms, as though he were begging to be picked up and carried around the house. Patrick looked to the hallway, knowing that the ambulance would arrive any minute. He took a deep breath, trying to prepare himself mentally to face the future.

"Where's my boy?" he heard his mother's wails coming from below. Patrick gritted his teeth as he listened to his father argue with her.

"Hold on. Don't yell. He needs some peace," his dad said. But instead of heeding his warnings, Patrick's mother ran upstairs, stomping her feet against the steps.

"Move!" She pushed his father aside the moment they reached the second floor. "Come here," she said to Delan. Without warning, she grabbed a hold of Patrick's collar and pulled him away. He tumbled toward the doorway and, much to his shock, he saw Delan clutching to her like she was the last person on earth. He dug his slender fingers deep into her robe while keeping his face close to her chest.

"Mom!" Patrick raised his voice, but instead of facing her usual anger, she appeared more loving than usual. While her emotions were strong, they weren't aggressive. Instead, she showed Delan a great deal of care as she cradled him. Patrick relaxed his shoulders, realizing that he overestimated the extent of his mother's anger.

The corner of Patrick's lips twitched. What else was his mom going to do? Was this only a brief instance of care? He watched her closely, prepared to intervene. However, his mother surprised him by singing a soft lullaby.

"Hush now, little baby, don't say a word. Mama's going to buy you a mockingbird."

Her gentle singing voice from years ago returned, making Patrick feel like he was stuck in a fever dream.

"How is she treating him?" Patrick's dad asked. After opening his mouth, Patrick shushed him. He pointed to his mother. Together, they watched the two of them interact. Meanwhile, the glazed look in his father's eyes surprised him as well. He stared onward, still concerned for his brother's well-being. Patrick never saw his dad gaze at his mother that way.

"Good. I was worried she'd scare him." They both glanced downward. "Stay downstairs and open the door the moment the paramedics arrive."

Patrick rushed downstairs with feathered footsteps. He sat beside the front door, waiting for the first responders. Meanwhile, he thought back to what may have transpired before Delan got home.

When did he leave?

He surmised it had to have been around 9:00 pm at least. Considering that he was deep into his gaming session and his parents would have gone to bed by then. 9:00 pm would've been the best time to sneak out. Not only that, but Delan appeared to have put more thought into his style than usual.

Patrick pursed his lips.

The girl. He must have left the house for his girlfriend.

But even if he figured out the exact time Delan left, that didn't answer who his girlfriend was or why meeting her had upset him so much. Patrick grumbled, getting lost in thought. Only when the first responders arrive did he snap back to reality. Their vehicles' lights shone through his window, and as soon as he opened the door, two paramedics came bounding up the driveway, followed by two police officers.

Patrick ushered them inside. While both EMTs and one officer spoke with his parents, one cop stayed behind to speak to Patrick. The man was relatively tall, and lanky. He spoke with the authority of someone who had been in his field for years.

"On the phone, your father claimed you were the one to find your brother, correct?"

"Yes."

The man reached out to shake his hand. "I'm Officer Hawthorne. Now, let's take a seat." For a moment, Patrick stood still, not knowing what to say.

"Hawthorne?" Patrick repeated.

The man nodded with his nametag further confirming this, underneath the kitchen lights. "Are you okay?"

Patrick nodded. "Yes, you just have the same name as one of my teachers. It surprised me."

The man remained silent as he sat at the dining table. Once he settled himself, he leaned forward and dragged a chair in front of him. He gestured toward it and Patrick sat down.

"How did you come across your brother?" he asked with a notepad in hand.

"I just got in bed when I heard him crying, so I went to check on him and realized he was upset. I tried to calm him and then I saw the knife in his hand. After that, I fought for it while yelling for my dad."

The officer nodded along with Patrick's account.

"Was he attacking you with the knife?"

Patrick crumbled the tablecloth underneath his hand. He flinched as his mother cried, repeatedly saying, "That's my baby," while they put Delan on a stretcher and carried him down the staircase. Soon, the distant sound of the gurney rolling down the pavement disappeared into the night.

"Hey, I still need to ask you a few questions."

The deputy snapped his fingers in front of Patrick's eyes.

"Right. He nicked me a little on the arm. It wasn't on purpose; he was just trying to escape my hold."

The man scrawled some notes on his pad.

"Let me see your arm."

Patrick rested his wrist on the table, which the cop glanced at briefly.

"Doesn't look too bad."

"It's not."

The man stood and walked toward the door.

"I'll be in touch shortly. Now, try your best to rest."

Despite it being direct and stilted, Patrick found solace in Officer Hawthorne's conversation. At least his demeanor made things quick and clear, unlike the chaos that had just transpired. Patrick leaned back in his chair while his parents shuffled out the door with their car keys in hand.

"Stay here. We're going to meet your brother at the hospital," his dad said reassuringly.

"Hold on. I want to go."

His mom shut the door without answering him, and the next thing he knew, they started the car. Patrick watched their headlights head off on the road.

Now what? He clenched his fist, knowing that sleep would be impossible to achieve. He went to his bedroom to retrieve his own car keys. He figured his parents would be away for quite some time, so the idea surfaced to drive to the residence of the one person he could think to speak with.

During a school event when he and his peers were tasked with selling baked pies, his former English teacher, Ms. Hawthorne, bought a sizeable chunk of them. Suddenly every student she'd ordered from had her home address. After the sale, some students tried to reach out to her, showing up at her residence as if she were a close friend. She turned them away, never hesitating to let everyone know how inappropriate it was. But as the memory soared through Patrick's head, he knew he had to show up at her doorstep. At least then, he'd be face-to-face with someone who had recently spent hours with Delan.

After jangling the keys with his fingers, he went outside and started his car. He let out a deep breath as he pulled out of his driveway, knowing Ms. Hawthorne would be even more wary about answering her front door at three in the morning. Within a mere ten minutes, Patrick arrived at her house. He stared up at the blue paint. As he slammed the brake into park, the front light on the porch flickered. A shadow swept past the curtain near the door, and a person quickly ducked out of sight.

Patrick zipped up his jacket and marched to the doorbell. He pressed the glowing white button. His body shivered as light footsteps approached. In no time at all, the door swung open, revealing Ms. Hawthorne with a surprised look on her face.

"Patrick?" she asked, fearfully. She parted the long strands of brown hair covering her eyes. While she appeared to be aged, her looks weren't completely devoid of beauty. Instead, she seemed to be stuck in a state of limbo. Between being freshly out of bed and coming home after a long night out.

"I need to talk to you," Patrick said.

"Do you have any idea what time it is?"

She stepped back slightly with her hand, closing the door.

"Ms. Hawthorne, please! I need to ask some questions about Delan!" Patrick's voice boomed down the road, but after his brief outburst, the neighborhood went silent again. "Please." He sniffled as he held back his tears.

"Okay." Finally, Ms. Hawthorne lowered her guard and opened the door wide, ushering him to come inside.

"T-thank you."

As Patrick entered her home, a rush of hot air consumed him.

"At first I thought you were angry, but I see that's not the case."

She gestured toward her couch. Immediately, Patrick jumped on it like an elated puppy. He sunk into the cushions, listening to the coffee maker brewing.

"What's going on?" she asked in a soft voice. Ms. Hawthorne sat down next to him, filling his nostrils with the faint scent of strawberries.

"Are you wearing perfume?" he asked, sniffing the air.

Ms. Hawthorne blushed.

"No," she said, sounding somewhat confused.

"My brother had the same smell on him." Patrick's voice trailed off and in the corner of his eye, he noticed a slight twitch on Ms. Hawthorne's lips.

"Is that so?"

"Yes, it was on him after school. It's everywhere in my car now."

"I see. I suppose the scent stuck with you then."

"You're right, I—"

"But what did you want to know about Delan?" she interjected.

Patrick sat upright to get down to business.

"Delan came home tonight and tried to kill himself."

Ms. Hawthorne gasped at his blunt deliverance.

"How is he?"

Patrick shook his head.

"He's alive. But he wouldn't tell me why he did what he did. That's why I wanted to ask if you noticed anything different about him lately." Patrick stared at her with weary eyes.

"I'm sorry about what happened." She hugged him tightly. And while Patrick was indeed grateful to be allowed her attention, he couldn't deny that he only wanted to hear what Ms. Hawthorne had to say about Delan.

"I'll get you some coffee to cheer you up." She got off the couch and strode toward the kitchen.

"Wait!" he called out. She stopped in her tracks and turned her head. "I just have a few questions."

Ms. Hawthorne gave a faint smile. "I know you're upset, but please, let me take care of you for a while."

"I'd rather—"

"Patrick, you need a break. I know you do."

"Look, I can handle what's going on. Let's just make this quick." His voice shook as he spoke, betraying his façade of appearing strong.

In the end, Ms. Hawthorne made her way toward the coffee stand and made him a fresh cup.

"Patrick, you're hurting. I know you are." Time stood still as he watched her gently pour the black liquid into a mug. And as the steam flew toward the ceiling, she poured another serving. "Yes, I'll gladly answer your questions, but you can't keep pushing yourself. For instance, your brother has told me how stressed you appeared these last few days."

Delan's eyes grew wide. "So, he opened up to you. What else did he say? Did he look depressed this last week?"

"I'll tell you everything I can. But please, take some time to care for yourself. Your brother clearly believed you were a strong man. But there's a difference between being strong and *having* to be strong." She whistled a tune while pouring the next drink, leaving Patrick to ponder her words.

She set her cup down on the end table beside her while passing Patrick the other beverage. Patrick took it, and for a moment, she grazed her fingertips against his knuckles.

"What's your first question?"

"Why was Delan in detention so often?"

Ms. Hawthorne cupped her hands snuggly around her mug. She closed her eyes for a few seconds as she recalled the events of the last few days.

"Well, your brother wasn't paying that much attention in class. He usually fell asleep during my lectures. At first, I did nothing. After all, teens go to school tired. It's just that after seeing him nod off consistently, I needed to use detention time to help him get caught up with his work."

Patrick took in what she said, realizing that his brother wasn't as miserable in her class as he thought he was.

"So, you only noticed he was tired? Nothing else?"

"Nope, I'm sorry. I wish I had more to say."

"Ms. Hawthorne, please . . ." Patrick's chest rose with the breath he took. "Did you see my brother talking to a girl? Any girl? Specifically, one who wore strawberry scented perfume?"

Ms. Hawthorne quickly shook her head. "Your brother speaks to everyone. Every girl and every boy."

"But did any of those girls wear that fruity perfume?"

Ms. Hawthorne hummed. "A lot do. That fragrance is quite common."

Patrick tightened his grip on the cushion. "That's not enough to go on."

Ms. Hawthorne eyed him. "What are you getting at?"

"It's just, I think he has a girlfriend, and she could be the source of his problems." After revealing his hypothesis, she spit out her coffee into her cup.

She gently lowered her drink to her lap.

"What makes you think that?"

"When I drove him home yesterday, I smelled that perfume on his clothes, so I guess he must have been around one girl in particular."

"Yes, but it's a very common scent."

Patrick nodded. "I know that, but there's more to it. When he tried to kill himself earlier, the smell was there again. The scent wasn't exactly the same, but I know it was perfume, and he looked as if he'd left the house earlier. I know he met up with someone."

Ms. Hawthorne's eyes lit up as though his words stirred something within her. "Did you notice anything else?"

"I saw someone outside my house before I heard Delan crying. I couldn't tell who it was, but I think it was a woman."

Ms. Hawthorne raised an eyebrow.

"You saw someone outside your house?"

"Yes, but I couldn't see their face or tell what car they were driving."

"Did you tell anyone else about this?"

Patrick shook his head. "I should have. One cop that responded to our 911 call questioned me. I should have told him about the car."

Ms. Hawthorne pulled him in for a hug. She rested her cheek on his shoulder, offering a sense of comfort that Patrick hardly experienced. "Who's the officer that talked to you? I'm guessing he'll be back to question you."

"Oh, he will be. It's strange to say, but his last name was 'Hawthorne.'"

Patrick's teacher lifted her head and looked him in the eyes. "You must have spoken to my brother!"

Patrick flinched.

"I'm sorry, what?" he asked, confused.

"He quite good at his job, you can trust him. I assure you; you can always talk to him about anything. He and I will be on your side."

She smiled at Patrick, who felt a great weight rise from his chest.

"Thank you," he whispered. As he finished his drink, Ms. Hawthorne tapped away on her phone.

"I just texted one of the substitute teachers to fill in for me today. You can stay here as long as you'd like."

Patrick blinked his eyes in surprise.

"Really?" he asked.

"Yes." She held her phone in front of him, clearly displaying the blue text showing her message. "I believe it's important to strike the perfect balance between my student's well-being and their academic performance. And right now, it seems like you could use all the support you can get."

A grin spread across Patrick's face. With her warm presence finally settling in, he found it feasible to loosen his shoulders.

"Thank you."

"Now, let's get back to it. You said you believe your brother was with someone tonight."

"Yes, that's right, and I want to find out who it was."

Ms. Hawthorne pursed her lips and looked forward as though she were contemplating deeply.

"I can't think of anyone. Also it isn't fair to point blame on any one student."

"Isn't there anything you can remember about my brother's mindset?" Patrick asked. "I just need something. Any bit of information to go on."

Ms. Hawthorne hummed quietly as she shuffled through a music playlist on her phone. She retrieved a remote from the coffee table at their feet and turned on a Bluetooth speaker. The soft strumming of a guitar filled the room.

"Perhaps you could think back to what you saw earlier. Is there anything about that woman's car that you recognize?"

"No. It was just a white Nissan Versa. I don't know anyone who drives that car."

At his statement, Ms. Hawthorne's eyes drifted toward a single door. The cold air seeping through the cracks told Patrick that it led to the garage.

"What's wrong?" he asked.

"Oh, it's nothing. I'm not very familiar with cars. But did you notice anything else? Maybe a license plate?"

Again, Patrick shook his head. No matter how much he recalled from his memory, not a single concrete piece of information came to him. Instead, a quiet voice with a mind of its own plagued him, calling him a failure.

"Here, I'll text my brother the details about the car and see if he can tell us who the driver is," Ms. Hawthorne offered.

"Really?"

"Yes. He can help."

"Okay," Patrick said without a hint of confidence. His eyes drooped low and his lips quivered.

"Hey, it's okay," Ms. Hawthorne said, as she up lifted his chin and bopped the tip of his nose. "We'll figure this out. But one more question. Can you describe the silhouette of the woman you saw?"

"She was quite thin. I wouldn't say skinny, but definitely more lean than normal. She also had long hair, just like you."

Ms. Hawthorne continued to type, slowly clutching her device closer to her chest with each passing second. "Thank you. This will help us tremendously."

Patrick leaned forward, eyeing her phone. "Can I see your text? I just want to make sure you're typing everything correctly."

Ms. Hawthorne frowned and shook her head. "Now, I'll gladly help you, but I still value some privacy."

"But I'm not planning to look through everything."

"I'm not saying you will. But I do speak to my brother about some rather personal issues I'm dealing with. Of course, it's still in our conversation history."

"Ms. Hawthorne, please I—"

"Don't you and Delan confide in each other every once in a while? You wouldn't want your conversation to be out in the open."

Her question forced Patrick's mouth shut. And when he failed to answer her, she nodded, knowing that he couldn't find a suitable rebuttal.

January 3rd

My Journal

Patrick tried one of our dad's beers on Christmas and New Year's. It's the first time I've seen him drunk and hopefully the last. He just went on and on about our old baby sitter. Calling her 'hot' and telling me how badly he would've 'banged' her. God, the way he talks now is so disgusting. Plus, she's seven years older than us. Isn't that weird? But I guess he sees nothing wrong with it. After all, he says it's every teenage boy's fantasy and that I probably have the same fantasies as well. What a joke.

Chapter 9

PRESENT

Patrick awoke in his car with the driver's seat tilted back. He lifted his head, scanning the interior, wondering how he got there.

The fall. The blood.

He fingered the back of his skull, finding nothing but his hair. With the gnarly gash gone, he tried to make sense of everything. He remembered the blue cloth, the rain, and the fall, but nothing else. Even Charlie wasn't there anymore.

"What the hell is going on?" Patrick muttered. The awful stench emanated from the back end of his vehicle and surrounded him. Patrick covered his mouth with his hand in case vomit spewed through his lips. He buckled down and clenched his stomach until the feeling to hurl passed. And once it did, he felt exhausted. With trembling palms, he shifted through his pockets for his car keys, only to turn-up empty-handed.

"Shit."

"You thought things could go back to the way they used to, didn't you?" Delan's voice spoke. In the rear-view mirror, his brother appeared, but when Patrick turned his head around, he saw nothing but the lifeless clothes he took with him. Patrick slammed his fist into the dashboard and grunted. As the strike spread a massive vibration through the vehicle, he heard Delan scoff. "I wish you didn't get angry so easily."

"I'm losing it," Patrick whispered to himself. He kept his eyes forward. The waves of the lake below crashed against the shore with a ferocity he never witnessed.

"Patrick, you thought I would love you like I used to, didn't you?"

Again, Delan's voice pierced his ears. His brother's figure appeared in the mirror again, but Patrick knew if he turned around it would vanish. So, he kept his head low, choosing to only take brief glances at his reflection. Patrick's knuckles turned white around the steering wheel. Meanwhile, the rain picked up speed, turning the ground around his vehicle into a large body of water.

"You'll always be my brother. You know that, right?"

"You're not real," Patrick whispered through gritted teeth.

"I love you." Delan's voice wavered as it spoke.

But Patrick shut his eyes and pretended to have never seen him. "Shut up."

"You know, while I was in the hospital, I always thought of you. I wanted you with me every minute and every second. I heard your voice at night when I tried to sleep, and I saw you in my dreams."

"You're not Delan."

"Patrick, my death is not your fault."

His brother's bold statement made him open his eyes wide. After staring at the mirror once again, he saw nothing and looking directly at the backseat didn't change anything either.

Delan, I . . .

Despite wanting nothing more than his brother's forgiveness, he couldn't grasp the situation entirely. Patrick stepped out of his car and clawed at the drenched pavement for his keys.

Where are they? He bit down on his lower lip, fighting back the urge to scream to the sky. He took in a deep breath. Mud and other bits of debris covered the road ahead, completely blocking him. Of course, even if he found his keys, what would be the point? The car wouldn't make it very far, anyway. He grumbled beneath his breath and headed toward the gas station, hoping to buy a poncho or anything to keep the water off him.

Can't freeze to death before making it to Skagway. He approached the small building. As he entered, he noticed the place was dark and barren. He flicked the light switch next to the empty counter, but nothing turned on.

"Luke?" Patrick called out. He stood still, expecting an answer. "Luke?" he said once more.

What's going on? He walked around the counter and the sight of the register shocked him. Instead of being a touch-screen device, it was an old till machine. Patrick peered down and lifted the radio that replaced Luke's smart phone. He gently twisted the knob with his fingers, only to jump when it returned to life. An old jazz tune played through the speakers while the sun cast a golden glow through the windows.

When looking outside, the parking lot beside the gas station appeared the same as it had always been—a gray rundown mess drenched in heavy rain. Patrick looked upward anxiously, trying to find the sun. He couldn't locate it. Instead, it was as if he was on a set with artificial lighting.

"Luke?" Patrick asked again in a shaky voice. He rummaged through the drawers of the till machine, hoping to find his cell phone or anything else that he recognized. He only found records containing dates of various purchases. All of which ended around 1952. Patrick threw the papers against the window, making them scatter apart in the air.

Then as each yellow piece floated downward, he saw Delan standing outside. The young boy smiled at him as though they were really facing each other. The rain silently battered his brother's shoulders, only confusing Patrick even more.

"You're not real!" Patrick yelled. Lightning struck in the background, filling the outside world with a bright flash. In the instant it happened, Delan disappeared. Patrick sighed heavily, then flinched when he heard the radio whirring to life. This time, it was Sofia's voice speaking to him.

"I wanted to turn all of my feelings into one story. A book for all of you to read."

Patrick chucked the device against the wall, making it shatter. Afterward, he stared at the broken pieces, feeling more satisfied than ever. He chuckled to himself like a madman, only to hold his breath when the debris slowly put themselves together as though time rewound itself. And when all was done, Sofia spoke once more: "My words are true, but can you say the same, *Patrick*?"

At the sound of his name, he stumbled backward, falling on his rear. He groaned as the pain consumed his bottom.

However, he quickly jumped up and bolted toward the exit. After leaving the gas station, he looked at the car, surprised to see Charlie waiting for him. The dog stood silently in the rain, as if suggesting that whatever had happened earlier was not meant to be.

"Charlie!" Patrick ran toward his furry companion. With the wind on his back, he ran faster than ever, until the rumbling of the ground sent him rocking. He flailed his arms, trying to maintain his balance, but to no avail. In the end, he fell to his knees. The earth's rocky vibrations weakened his arms, turning them into noodles. Meanwhile, the trees and cliffs shifted until the land became completely flat. Patrick kept his forehead touching the wet concrete to avoid gazing at the horrific sight.

You have no right to exact vengeance on others! a voice whispered in his ear like a snake hissing.

Patrick covered the sides of his face with his palms.

Look your brother in the eye and tell him what you did!

As the voice grew in intensity, Patrick's pulse pounded. Charlie's low growl faded away until Patrick heard nothing more than his blood pumping through his veins.

Wake up and face what you've done.

With that statement, Patrick threw his head back and screamed from physical pain. It felt as though thousands of daggers stabbed deep into his abdomen.

"What's going on?!" The inside of his throat tore apart as he raised his pitch. His head throbbed with a gnawing pain that seemed to come from the inside of his skull. And as the pain continued, he fell over, unmoving, and put into a deep sleep.

January 5th

MY JOURNAL

Patrick and I got into a fight earlier. I caught him watching some stuff on his computer. I don't want to go into a lot of detail, but he got mad at me for accidentally barging in. He tried to explain that Khen sent him videos of those men as a joke. At first, I didn't know he was watching videos of men. I mean, some of the tabs he had opened were of women too, but regardless, why get mad at me? Was it because I walked in on him? I told him I'd knock next time. Even then, the way he looked at me was scary. I've never seen him so angry before. And the strange thing is, I swore I heard him crying a few minutes after I left.

Chapter 10

PAST

For the rest of the night, Patrick and Ms. Hawthorne spoke fondly of Delan. Patrick told stories of their childhood while Ms. Hawthorne listened intently with the occasional comment. After a dozen stories, Patrick's eyes felt heavy, and once he yawned, Ms. Hawthorne helped him off the couch. She gently held him up, placing her hands on his upper arms. She giggled at the sight of him, making his face turn red.

Patrick's mind went back to the pictures of his schoolmates on social media. He wondered what they would say if they saw him and Ms. Hawthorne like this. The question made him feel disgusted. With Delan recently attempting to take his life, Patrick tried his best to clench his fist, ready to punch himself.

Being a pervert at a time like this?

But despite that, he couldn't deny butterflies in his stomach. Ms. Hawthorne's soft hands and willingness to help were the perfect combination for fostering a safe environment.

In his grogginess, he let out a faint smile, feeling relieved that he found himself attracted to a woman, rather than a man or some boy in his class. Still, a small pool of guilt lingered within.

What am I? he asked himself. Would this feeling be fleeting? One that would disappear within the coming hours? After which, he would question his attractions again. And why should he fear being gay?

The questions made Patrick want to bite down on his wrist as punishment. He knew something was off. That maybe, this wasn't pure attraction, but a sensation coming from a feeling of safety.

"Are you still there?" Ms. Hawthorne asked playfully. Patrick nodded, and she placed her palm on his cheek. He grunted as he took in her warmth and from his distorted vision, he swore she made an odd movement. One that brought her closer than he expected. But the moment he opened his eyes fully, Ms. Hawthorne flinched. "Easy there. You almost fell."

"I'm sorry." Patrick scoffed at himself mentally for thinking Ms. Hawthorne leaned into him.

"I'll drive you home," she said, carrying him to the front door.

"How do you know where I live?"

"Easy. School directories. Plus, every teacher has emergency contact information of all the students in their class."

"Really?"

She pressed a button on her keys, which lifted the garage door. While her car remained a blurry mess, Patrick couldn't deny that it looked familiar. It was polished and relatively small. His blurred vision made the car a sparkling specter and soon, he figured he must've seen the same model at a car show some years ago. But what was the model? After all, if he had all the money in the world, he'd buy another vehicle to replace his beat-up mess.

January 12th

MY JOURNAL

Patrick and I haven't fought in a while. The problem is that we haven't talked in a while either. Every day after school, I see him lock himself away in his bedroom. I assume he's playing some games, since his keyboard is sounding like a typewriter. But that's exactly what makes it worse. Knowing that he's so close, yet he feels so far away. If he doesn't want to come out and talk to me, maybe I should try writing him a letter. That'll get his attention. I hope. Even Dad is getting worried. He says Patrick is more withdrawn than usual. Of course, he suggested seeking a counselor for him, but Mom didn't agree. She says he's not insane, just a little shy. But why would getting help make him insane?

Chapter 11

PRESENT

By the time Patrick awoke to the pattering of rain on his face, Luke was standing over him with his hand extended outwards.

"What the hell happened?" Patrick asked. He looked at Luke, not knowing if he was real or another hallucination. But when the young man shook his shoulder, Patrick felt the hardness of his fingers stabbing into his sleeve. "Where have you been all this time?"

Luke grunted as he lifted Patrick to his feet. "I just got out of the break room and noticed you lying here. Did you fall?" He dragged him back inside the gas station, where he pulled out a chair by the counter. Once Patrick rested on the cushion, he eyed the spotless surface that now held a till with a touch screen and many shelves housing Luke's belongings along with his cellphone.

"The notes? The radio?" Patrick whispered.

Luke narrowed his eyes and leaned closer. "What are you saying?"

"You weren't here. There were notes and a radio." Patrick spoke softly while running his fingers across the countertop. Luke pulled himself back.

"I'm going to get you an ice pack, but if you keep acting that way, I'm going to call an ambulance."

"Ambulance . . . " Patrick repeated.

Luke quietly walked away, disappearing through the cooler door. In the meantime, Patrick rested his chin on his hand. Just like before, the rain was still present. In fact, it seemed to be slightly harsher. With the parking lot completely devoid of life, Patrick's mind wandered to various conclusions about what took place.

Charlie.

His eyes popped open. Where'd that little mutt go? He left the comfort of his chair and headed toward the window. Upon looking out, he realized that Charlie really was gone. Not a single remanent of Charlie's existence remained except for Patrick's busted trunk.

"Here." Luke handed Patrick an ice pack.

After placing it on the back of his head, he followed Luke's lead and sat down beside the counter. "Where is he?" Patrick grumbled.

"Where's who?"

"The dog. Where's Charlie?"

A puzzled expression appeared on Luke's face.

"Listen, if you don't stop acting like a lunatic, I'll call 911. Considering your confusion, I don't want you walking around."

"No!"

Luke jumped when Patrick slammed his hand on the table. "I was with Charlie. That husky that came into the store earlier. Where is he?"

"Patrick, he left the store after I shoved him away. Don't you remember?"

"I know that, but after he left the store, he waited by my car."

"I didn't see him out there. Just you sitting in your vehicle watching videos on your phone."

Patrick leaned back in his chair and sighed.

"I'm losing it."

Luke patted his shoulder. "Just sit here, alright? Take advantage of that ice pack and we'll see how you feel then."

Afterward, he began sketching in his notebook again, still acting and speaking like an alien imitating a person. Patrick glanced at the pages, almost passing out at the sight of it. Next to his current drawing was a detailed sketch of Patrick sitting in his car and being completely engrossed in staring at his phone screen. Luke went as far as drawing small bits of Sofia's face in the tiny square.

"Luke, how long was I in the car?"

"I'd say about twenty minutes. It took me seventeen to draw a rough sketch and three more to make sure I got it right. Afterward, I saw you lying out there."

"You consider that to be a rough sketch?" Patrick asked rhetorically. Luke chuckled.

"Maybe I'm just a perfectionist, but to me, it's not enough."

"What else do you have in that book?"

Patrick sat upright as Luke positioned the notebook in between them. Both boys leaned in closer to view the artwork. Luke began on the first page, which depicted a man with a scar over his cheek. He held a mean gaze as he looked outward over the cliffside.

"This was a weird guy. A dangerous one too. A couple of days after he stopped by, I found a news story about him being arrested for aggravated assault. Thankfully, he didn't kill me."

Luke flipped through more pages, stopping at a beautiful woman with hair cut to her shoulders. "To be honest, I loved drawing her. In fact, I drew her a lot."

He gestured to more pages of the woman's face, each showcasing her at a different angle. "She visited me so many times. I was starting to think I was some sort of stud. But turns out she was a predator. Some cops questioned me three days after she left for good. Apparently, she groomed some little boys, and I guess she thought I was a minor."

Luke heaved a heavy sigh and looked out the window. In the meantime, Patrick eyed each drawing carefully. "So, you really get some horrible people stopping by."

"Yup, it's unfortunate. But I'm just glad you're normal. I mean, you are, right?"

Patrick averted his gaze. "No, not really."

"Okay, but even if you're weird, it's not in some criminal way, right?" He gave a nervous laugh, which Patrick didn't entertain.

"Nothing illegal. I'm just an asshole. I didn't treat my brother right."

"A bit of sibling rivalry?"

"Not just rivalry, but pure negligence as well." Patrick rested his elbows on the counter, still trying to take in everything. He knew Luke was real and Charlie, but what happened in the time he left the building after meeting Luke? Were those events fake? Patrick flinched at the sudden onset of a headache.

"Woah. Here." Luke handed a napkin. He pointed at Patrick's nose. Patrick swiped his nostril and found blood was pouring out of his right nostril.

Patrick pinching his nose, but he was distracted from the nosebleed. He wanted to play the most recent video he saw uploaded by Sofia. In it, she immediately went into depth about the story she was writing.

The bluntness of her words and diction made it clear it was a fictional narrative with some of her personal experiences woven in. However, one thing that really caught Patrick's attention was the way she described a woman's voice. Apparently, it sounded like a serpent, much like the voice he heard earlier.

"Do you like horror?" Luke asked, breaking Patrick's concentration.

"I never really read horror novels. I'm only listening to her because my brother did."

"Oh, I see. I looked into her content after you mentioned it. She seems like a depressing person. She is always talking about guilt, redemption, and her dysfunctional family life. It's the macabre mixed with tragedy."

Patrick paused the video and turned to Luke.

"This sounds crazy, but what if the setting in her novel is true?"

Luke shook his head. "That is crazy. Yes, she said that it incorporates parts of her life, but don't you think it'd be more reasonable to assume the main character is modeled after her? Maybe not as a shameless self-insert, but as someone with similar strengths and flaws."

Patrick nodded. "Maybe. But I can't shake off this feeling that the town she mentioned is real. Like I said, it's crazy."

Luke scribbled in his notebook again. This time, he drew Charlie completely from his memory. Patrick leaned closer to get a better view of his drawing. While Luke's hand effortlessly glided across the page, his face showed pure focus.

"What's that?" Patrick pointed at the faint outline of a garbage bag sticking out of his trunk. Within the sketch, Charlie sat patiently by the rear of the vehicle, yet with the trunk drawn slightly open, Patrick noticed the large bag.

"I saw it when I glanced over at him. This might sound rude, but what kind of trash is in your trunk?"

Patrick scooted away from him, feeling offended. "It's not trash. It's my brother's clothes."

"Does he not wash after himself?" Luke said sarcastically.

"Don't talk about him like that."

For a moment, the two of them made eye contact. Patrick noticed the creases on Luke's forehead while he was confident Luke caught wind of the pain in his eyes. "Sorry." He went back to driving his pencil into the white paper. A small piece of graphite broke off and rolled toward the edge of the book.

"Damn."

While Luke knelt below the register to grab another pencil, Patrick noticed the broken piece leaving behind a black trail like the darkness of Raven feathers. The long line it left behind turned jet black and slowly spread throughout the outline like blood vessels.

"Luke!" Patrick yelled. When the employee stood straight, he raised an eyebrow.

"What?"

Patrick pointed at the sketchbook, which was completely devoid of the black lines he saw merely a few seconds ago.

"Is the drawing really that bad?" Luke dusted off the graphite shavings and presented it to Patrick. "Take another look. It can't be that bad, right?" He spoke fast and with a great sense of curiosity.

"Never mind. I'm just going to lie down." Patrick trotted toward the doorway, much to Luke's dismay. When the young man warned him to watch his step, Patrick simply nodded and waved goodbye.

As he strode across the pavement, the fog momentarily cleared, giving him sight of a small island in the middle of the lake. Small bits of garbage revealed themselves before the weather became unbearable again. In no time at all, he got into his car. Patrick slumped in the driver's seat, finally giving himself a chance to rest his shoulders.

Maybe I am just insane.

He recounted the hours of sleep he had the previous night, lifting only five fingers. From there, he closed his eyes, hoping that a nap would take away the confusion.

"There's a cycle to be broken here," Delan's voice said. Patrick's eyes shot open, only to realize that he was alone in his car.

Not again.

He titled his seat back, hoping to make it comfortable enough to drift himself into a deep sleep, but when he closed his eyes, he heard Delan speak. "All you've been feeling is guilt and then anger. You need to break this cycle. But it can only happen when you decide to walk away."

Patrick kept his eyes shut, telling himself that he was merely hallucinating his brother's voice. He took in a deep breath, finally feeling his arms go limp. The tension in his ankles, wrist, and shoulders gradually disappeared, giving way to pure relaxation.

February 14th

MY JOURNAL

Man, it's been so long since I've written anything. I practically had to clean out my entire room just to find my journal, but I really just need to get something off my chest. Ms. Hawthorne has been getting much too close to me. The way she pressed her chest against my arm while I'm in class makes me want to wash my entire body until my skin flies off. I want to tell someone, but I'm scared. She's the adult here and so many others like her. Teachers, students, and parents. Will they trust me? If only Patrick were here for me. Sure, he's only across the hall from me, but the way he talks to Khen. The things they say about how obsessed they are with women. Any woman. It could be a girl in their class or it could be someone older, like our babysitter. The way Patrick drools over her social media posts makes me want to vomit. Can't he see that he's trying too hard? Why is he so obsessed with appearing 'cool' or some other bullshit like that? He's the first one I thought of opening up to, but with the way he looks at those girls, I'm afraid he'll give me a pat on the back. That he'll congratulate me for 'bagging' Ms. Hawthorne, or worse, he'll get jealous and cut me off.

Chapter 12

PAST

Patrick awoke the next morning on his couch. Sunshine blasted through his window, forcing him to squint his eyes as he rose from the cushions. He thought back to last night, wishing that it was nothing more than a nightmare. The sharp scrape of his car keys against his leg reminded him he still had to retrieve his vehicle. However, when he stuck his hand in the little fold, his fingers pressed against a sticky note.

Here's my phone number. Text me when you want to pick up your car.

Patrick smirked at it. The knowledge that he had Ms. Hawthorne to confide in during this turbulence in his life comforted him. He quickly got up and strode toward his parents' bedroom. After pressing his ear against the door, he clearly heard his father's deep snores, letting him know they wouldn't miss him for at least a few hours.

Can you help me pick up my car? he texted his teacher.

Yes. Her reply came almost instantly. The speed at which his phone buzzed sent a shockwave throughout his body. Even Khen didn't answer him that fast. The oddity of it all made his stomach queasy.

Butterflies? Patrick condemned himself for thinking like a child. While students occasionally developed a crush on their educators, he hated himself for feeling such things at a time like this. He sat beside the window, waiting for Ms. Hawthorne to arrive. He decided that once he had his car back, he would drive home and ask his parents where Delan had been admitted.

I'm waiting outside.

Patrick peeked out the window and saw Ms. Hawthorne sitting inside her car. Oddly enough, her vehicle didn't appear as polished as it was the previous night. A sight which Patrick attributed to his weariness.

I'm coming.

He ran down the walkway, straight for Ms. Hawthorne's car. Her eyes opened wide, as if she didn't expect to see him break into a sprint.

"Thank you," he said. She nodded and opened the door. Once he buckled his seatbelt, she wasted no time in getting him to her house.

"Hold on, before you go, I want to talk to you," she said as she parked in her driveway.

"What is it?"

"I'm willing to help you in any way I can, but please, keep our meetings between us."

"Why?" His voice trailed off as the wind tapped against the windows.

"Because our 'relationship' seems odd. I'm only here to provide comfort and help you get through this ordeal, but others won't see that. They'll see a grown woman spending too much time alone with one of her students. Do you understand what I'm getting at?"

Patrick pursed his lips. "I understand."

He rubbed his chin, considering what their actions looked like to the rest of the world. While he initially came to her for help, he also couldn't deny the raw attraction he felt.

In that moment, as the sun loomed over them, the way her hair shined made him want to lean forward and kiss her. But before his body acted on instinct, her smile reminded him of the way his mother used to care for him. Suddenly, her talks of stranger danger seeped into his mind, making him brush the thought away.

Ms. Hawthorne wouldn't hurt me. He suppressed his feelings and let out a deep cough.

"Are you telling me the truth?" she asked sternly.

"Yes."

At his response, she smiled once more, and Patrick quickly backed away to keep himself grounded.

She put her hand slightly above his knee and said, "Thank you."

Patrick shifted uncomfortably in his seat, telling himself that she was simply a touchy person.

It doesn't mean anything, he told thought to himself as he stared at her hand. Yet he couldn't deny how much he wanted it to mean something. He bit down on the inside of his cheek to keep himself from grinning.

"Well, there's your car," she gestured.

"Oh, right."

Patrick awkwardly shuffled out of her vehicle, wishing the car ride was longer. He pushed away his own heart's internal pleas to stay, and waved goodbye as he walked toward his vehicle. Once he ignited the engine, he stomped the gas pedal to rush home before he completely lost his mind.

In the meantime, he tried to shift his focus back to Delan. Should he wake up his parents or give them time to sleep? He certainly wanted to visit his brother's hospital immediately, but considering his parents' stress, maybe it was best to wait a few hours. However, by the time he got home, he already made up his mind.

Sorry.

Without hesitation, he entered his house and opened the door to his parents' bedroom.

"Dad?" he asked, shaking his father's shoulder.

"What?" his dad grumbled back, barely awake.

"What hospital was Delan taken to?"

His eyes rolled upward as he stuttered. "It-it's . . . we'll visit him soon, I promise."

"Alright, but I want to call then."

His dad nodded and reached over to the lamp, where a note was laid below it.

"Dial this phone number."

For the first time since he was a child, he gave his dad a tight hug. The man's large hand patted his back as Patrick took in a deep breath.

"I love you," he whispered.

"Your mother and I love you too, and your brother."

When Patrick receded from his dad's embrace, he watched him roll onto his back, ready to continue his slumber. Without making a sound, he left the room and sat on the couch, stabbing the phone number inro the on-screen keypad. The phone rang incessantly until a woman answered.

And without waiting for her to speak, Patrick opened his mouth.

"Can I speak to Delan? Delan Colt. I'm his brother, Patrick Colt."

"Give me just a moment."

On the other end of the line, she flipped through stacks of papers until she made an "aha" sound.

"Can you get Delan? His brother's on the phone. I've already confirmed that he's one of the contacts listed here," she said to her coworker.

Patrick held his breath as he recognized the faint footsteps of Delan approaching. From there, they transferred the call.

"Hello," his brother said. His voice was hoarse, as though he spent the entire night crying.

"Hi." Patrick swallowed hard, not knowing what to say.

"What do you want?" Delan sniffled.

"I just wanted to check in on you. See how you've been so far."

"Well, I tried to kill myself last night and now I'm in a psych ward. I feel bad."

"Understandable."

Patrick bit down on his lip to stop himself from groaning. He hated himself for not knowing what to say. Deep down, he felt like an idiot, deserving of a dunce cap for asking his brother how he was doing.

Of course, he feels bad.

He paused, internally debating whether he should dive into his plans to find the girl that caused all of this. But then again, he knew his brother felt horribly exhausted. "Listen, Delan . . . How long can you stay on the phone?"

"No one here is going to stop me in the middle of a phone call."

"I'm not asking if they'll stop you. I want to know if you're willing to stay awhile. I need to know if you want to talk to me."

A few seconds passed in silence. Only Delan's faint breathing seeped through the speaker. "Yes." It was a simple statement, but one that made Patrick's heartbeat faster.

"I want you to know that I'm sorry. I've been such a jackass. If I had known everything that was happening in your life, I'd have done anything to change it. I—"

"You don't need to apologize. None of this is your fault."

Despite his kind words, Patrick didn't sense any hint of emotion in his brother's voice, as if he had already died.

"Okay, but I promise you, I'll fix this. I'll find whoever is responsible."

Delan sighed. "Can't you leave this alone for now?"

"What? No, Delan, whoever hurt you last night needs to pay for it!"

"So that's why you're calling me? You just want to find out who I was with?" he asked in a snarky tone. "Mom, Dad, and the cops already questioned me about this. Can't all that stay buried in the past?"

"Delan, I'm sorry I—"

After one loud scream, the line went dead. Patrick buried his face in his hands. Of course Delan wasn't ready to talk about the previous night. Patrick stabbed himself with his fingernail.

I should've kept things fun and caring.

Amidst his frustration, he texted Khen, getting a sudden and intense craving to release some stress.

Hey, any updates on the party later?

He waited eagerly for Khen to respond to his text.

It starts at 6:00 pm. I'm not sure when it'll end, so we might be there all night.

Fine with me. There's going to be alcohol, right?

Khen's next message took considerably longer to type. But once he sent his message, his tone changed.

What's with the change in attitude? You seemed pretty hesitant last night.

I don't care anymore. All I want to do is get completely wasted. I'll even take a girl home if I can.

Hell yeah. I don't know what's gotten into you, but it's about time you loosen up.

Patrick smirked at his screen before tossing his phone aside to take a nap. Whether or not his parents wanted him home, he knew he'd get to that party and drink his worries away.

February 16th

My Journal

I tried to talk to Patrick about it, and of course, it didn't work out. It was the first time he let me into his room in about a month, but I could tell he didn't want to talk about anything sad or serious. Still, at the very least, I got to play some games with him. We hadn't done that in a while. I don't know what's changed, or if he'll stay this way, but it's nice to see him happy again. Of course, his eyes were bloodshot, and he smelled like a skunk. But I don't know what that's about. If he's happy, I'm happy. Hopefully, we can spend more time like this and maybe next time he won't eat two bags of chips all on his own, and let me have some.

Chapter 13

PAST

For most of the day, Patrick lay on his couch, scrolling through his device and glaring at his parents as they spoke to Delan over the phone. The way they effortlessly engaged with him made Patrick hate himself even more.

While he felt responsible for Delan's frustration earlier, he couldn't deny the pain of jealously when he noticed how long his parents had talked to him. But at the very least, now that they were preoccupied, he could snatch his car keys without being noticed. He remained stone-face as he went toward the door. Suddenly, he felt the air around him shift when his mother turned her head.

"Where are you going?" she asked.

"To a school event." Patrick quickly shut the door behind him and drove a lonely road to a nearby lake. He wondered what Delan was up to. Was the boy suffering in silence, tormented by his own thoughts and negative experiences, or was he slowly recovering?

The questions hammered into Patrick's skull, and he flinched as though the anguish manifested itself into an actual weapon. A weapon that swung downward, cracking his skull into pieces.

But soon, he shut himself off. The road faded away and a few hours later; he found himself sitting in front of a fire. The flames reflected in his irises. He dangled a beer bottle in front of him as he clenched his teeth.

"Hey!" Khen said, sitting next to him. Without saying anything, Patrick took another sip. "Look over there." His friend pointed at a group of students dancing around a speaker. The music blasted through the air like a muffled mess.

"So what?" Patrick asked.

"What do you mean, so what? You've just been sitting here, staring into that fire!"

"Give me some time."

"Time? You've been sulking all night!" He gripped Patrick by the wrist and tugged upward. Without dropping his drink, Patrick resisted against Khen's pull until they finally lost contact with one another. "Can't you stop being such a downer? We came here to let loose."

After one loud burp, Patrick tossed his bottle to the side.

"Look, you can go on ahead. I'll join you later."

"You said that an hour ago." Khen folded his arms across his chest while staring down menacingly. His fingers twitched as though he were holding himself back from strangling Patrick. "Those girls are pretty hot, aren't they?"

Patrick nodded without turning away from the pit. To him, the drink was all he needed. No one else at the party mattered. Only the booze to help calm himself during his time as an amateur sleuth.

"You didn't even look."

Khen spat on the ground.

"You caught me there," Patrick said sarcastically. "I'm not interested."

"Oh really? Is that why Delan has a girlfriend, and you don't?"

Patrick looked up at Khen with his nose distorted in anger. "I have a lot to deal with, so just leave me be!"

"Then stop acting like a pussy and join me!"

Patrick shook his head and lazily threw his arm over the lid of the cooler. He picked at the handle, trying to get it open.

"Go away," he muttered.

Khen kicked the icebox, sending clumps of dirt flying. Every bottle inside rolled across the ground toward the edge of the forest where the cliff waited. "You're pathetic, you know that? I bet your brother would've had the balls to go for it."

At his comment, Patrick jumped to his feet and gripped Khen by the collar. He pressed his face forward, getting their noses closer together.

"You don't know what Delan is going through, so keep him out of your goddamn mouth!" Patrick let go and turned on his heels to retrieve the drinks.

"Well, what has he been through? You've barely spoken to me since we got here."

Patrick turned around and marched back to his old friend.

"He tried to kill himself last night, and it's all because of that mysterious girlfriend of his."

For a moment, Khen stood still in shock.

"Well, at least he won't die a virgin." He mocked.

"Is sex the only thing on your mind? Can't you think of anything else?"

"What? Am I wrong for acting like a man?"

Patrick chucked a beer at him, making it shatter against a tree trunk.

"I--I can't believe I was stupid enough to want to impress you."

"What was that?" Khen chuckled to himself and let his laughter grow louder as Patrick revealed his weary face.

"I've been so stupid."

"You've always been an idiot."

Patrick ground his teeth together before leaping forward. He struck Khen in the mouth, digging his knuckles deep into his teeth. After he hit the ground, the rest of the partygoers watched the spectacle. "Shut the hell up about all this 'man stuff!' Why should anyone take advice from you?"

Suddenly, he imagined Khen's face replaced with his own as he sent a flurry of punches downward.

Why? Why was I so dumb?

Patrick knew now just how pointless it was to change himself by doing such trivial things. From sitting in the parking lot revving his engine, trying to smoke cigarettes, and ogling over his female peers on social media, how could he try to become someone he's not when he didn't even know who he was?

Patrick slowly got back to his feet. At first, he kept his gaze downward, feeling a sense of accomplishment for silencing his former friend. But after Khen wiped the blood off his lip, he focused his eyes on Patrick.

Without warning, he jumped to his feet and dashed toward him, laying his hands on his shoulders and bringing them both to the ground. As soon as he mounted Patrick, he began an onslaught of punches to the boy's face. Meanwhile, Patrick desperately clawed upward, trying to get ahold of Khen's wrist.

Battered and bruised, Patrick accidentally sliced Khen's eye with his nail. His friend toppled over, holding the right side of his face. A tear dripped out of his uninjured socket.

"Why do I even spend time with you?" Patrick asked.

"Because you have no one else."

With that, Khen walked away, disappearing into the crowd.

Patrick took a deep breath and sat by the flames, holding his hands in front of him. As the pain of the fight stung his face, he found solace in the warm fire. He thought back to the events of the previous day. Whoever drove Delan home that night would be the key to solving this mystery.

Thin, with shoulder length hair. It wasn't much to go on, so he felt a sharp pain in his chest, being unable to create a list of suspects. In his moment of grief, he took out his phone to call Delan.

"Hello, who is this?" a woman on the other line asked.

"I'm Patrick, Delan's sibling. I should be an approved caller." The woman loudly ruffled through sheets of paper, before breaking off.

"I apologize, but it seems you are no longer on the list." Patrick's chest tightened.

Not on the list? Did he take me off? Patrick bit down on his tongue, knowing that lashing out at the staff wouldn't win him any favors. So, he simply said "goodbye," and hung up.

Afterward, he put his phone back in his pocket to sulk. He wiped a tear that escaped, only to flinch at the blaring blue and red sirens approaching the forest.

He and everyone else at the party must have missed the sounds, thinking it was part of someone's music, but after the familiar red and blue lights of patrol vehicles appeared, everyone turned to run. While the drinks had dampened his cognitive functions, Patrick still found the strength to escape. He tumbled down the hillside toward the lake that awaited him. After he heard the barking of police dogs, he jumped into the freezing body of water, swimming across it, toward a larger hill. In the background, he heard officers yelling, commanding everyone to stand still.

He flailed his arms forward and ducked underneath the surface when the beam of a flashlight flew overhead. Once all was clear, he made his way forward, finally coming to the hill. He slapped his muddy hands on the rocks to get a good grip and heaved himself upward, fighting against the pain in his muscles. Only when he reached the top did he take a breath. In the end, he found himself in the vacant parking lot of a gas station. Luckily for him, the pumps were empty. Not a single person was there to report him. However, his relief faded when he realized the water soaked his mobile phone.

Damn it. He stumbled into the gas station, making eye contact with the cashier. An older gentleman who gave no reaction.

"Can I use your phone?" Patrick asked him nervously.

The man eyed him.

"Sure, but make it quick. I've seen enough bullshit at my job already." He laid his cellphone on the counter.

Patrick quickly swiped it away and racked his brain for Ms. Hawthorne's phone number. After dialing it, he waited, tapping his foot along with the buzzing of the phone.

"Who is this?" she asked.

"Oh, thank God. Listen, I-I need your help."

"Patrick, is that you? What's going on?"

Patrick took a gulp. "I screwed up. Look, please help me. I can't go to my parents with this. They have enough to deal with already."

Ms. Hawthorne loudly sighed on the other end.

"Fine, but first tell me what happened."

Patrick's lips quivered as the pain in his chest begged him not to tell the truth.

"I went to a party, I got into a fight, I got wasted and someone called the cops, so I ran away."

"Jesus. Do you know how much trouble I'd be in for helping you?"

"You're right. I'm sorry I asked." Patrick slumped his shoulders, ready to give up all hope.

"That doesn't mean I'm leaving you to fend for yourself. Tell me where you are, and I'll get you."

Patrick eyed the sign beside the glass door. Mounted on the window read "Jay's Station."

"I'm at a gas station. It's named 'Jay's Station.'"

"Stay right there." After that, she ended the call, and Patrick awkwardly handed the device back to the cashier.

"Thank you," he said.

The man shook his head disappointedly.

"Wait outside for your ride. You're making the floors filthy." He spoke with an aura of hostility that made Patrick speed walk out the door. And once the cold air hit his face, he sat on the curb, shivering.

????

MY JOURNAL

I woke up today thinking it was Friday, but when I saw my mom watching TV in the living room, I realized I was wrong. Her shifts are always in the afternoon on Thursdays. Can you imagine missing an entire day? Anyway, I suppose it's because I tried some of what Patrick was trying. The redness of his eyes, the way he smelled like a skunk. It all makes sense now. I wonder where he got the pot from, especially since it's illegal where we live, but I can't help wanting to try some. With everything that's happened. Ms. Hawthorne pushing herself on to me and Patrick ignoring me. I think if I tried being more like him, he'd like me more, right? Still, I wish he'd start looking my way again. Not like yesterday when he only did because he was high. I want him to act like my big brother again. I guess I'll try to make moves on Ms. Hawthorne. Who cares if I hate it? I should learn to love it, right? I think that's what Patrick would do.

Chapter 14

PRESENT

Patrick jumped upright at the sound of the car radio playing static. He blinked a few times before his vision returned to normal.

As the blur faded away and the gray outside world became clear, he realized it was still raining. Not only that, but the sun remained in the same position.

He looked at the digital clock on his dashboard. The tiny numbers on the top right corner, showing each passing second, didn't move. He slapped it, trying to see if it would work again, but did that really matter? What if the radio never worked at all? What if it was always broken? He couldn't shake off what Luke told him. About finding him on the ground with Charlie nowhere to be seen.

"Finally awake?" Delan said. His voice caught Patrick's attention, but as always, he wasn't there. The temperature in the car dropped significantly, causing Patrick to shudder.

You're not real, he told himself, to stay sane. He shoved his keys in the ignition, intending to fiddle with the heater, but when the car didn't turn on at all, he cussed and punched the knobs.

He slammed his back into the chair and took slow, steady breaths to regain his composure. The radio whirred to life once more, bombarding him with the voices of various talk show host and musicians. After sinking his knuckles into it one more time, it stopped on one radio station.

"Next on our true crime podcast, we'll be discussing the murder of--" The audio cut off before they could name the victim. Patrick ripped his keys out of the ignition and stomped toward the gas station, hoping that Luke would ease his mind. On his way there, he caught wind of the sign dangling beside the door. He hadn't noticed it before, since it remained shut off, but reading the name seemed familiar. Patrick stared at it for a while, only to be brought back to the present moment when Luke waved at him through the glass.

Patrick let out a smile and walked inside. "Well, that was fast," he said.

"It didn't feel like it."

Luke chuckled. "A one-minute nap is all it takes to get you fully rested?"

"One minute?" Patrick eyed the wall clock behind the counter and just as Luke stated, only a minute passed since he closed his eyes for a nap. He made his way toward the counter to sit beside Luke.

"Listen, I'm kind of scared, to be honest," Patrick blurted out.

Luke looked up from his sketchbook and set his pencil down. "About what? The thunder?"

"No. Ever since I got here, everything has felt so off. I'm just confused."

"Off?" Luke pushed his drawings aside and kept his attention on Patrick.

"Well, time feels weird. To me, that nap felt like a couple hours, but as you said, it was only a minute long. And then there's Charlie." Patrick wanted to say more, but he feared he'd scare Luke away. After all, he knew the kind of reaction he'd get if he confessed to hearing his brother's voice and the voice of the mysterious woman.

"Being out here in the middle of nowhere will do that to you. But about Charlie . . . he stops by now and then. Maybe you saw him, and I wasn't paying attention."

"Yeah, maybe." Patrick fingered the wallet in his pocket and grabbed a snack in front of the register. He dropped it on the counter and Luke instinctively put his card into the card reader. After the transaction, Patrick bit into it, savoring the chocolate.

"You like those things too?" he asked.

"Never tried them before."

Luke handed him another one. "Don't worry about paying for it. I can spare an extra dollar."

Patrick giggled like a little kid as he thanked him. While Luke went back to his drawing, Patrick wondered if staying here was a mistake. Leaving his hometown was heartbreaking, especially with how much his parents cared for him since Delan's death.

Still, Patrick felt he deserved some time to himself.

I found his 'girlfriend.' He thought back to the one person who pushed his brother over the edge. But just before he brought her face to his mind, a bolt of lightning struck in the distance.

"Damn!" Luke yelped.

Patrick followed his gaze, noticing the flashes in the distance. With the storm picking up, he figured it'd be best to stay inside the station.

Patrick quietly took another bite, only to drop his food when the power went out.

"Shit!" he muttered. But just as soon as it went out, the lights flickered on. "Luke . . ." The counter beside him was vacant. Patrick gasped and jumped out of his chair.

What the hell? The storm grew stronger, with a howling wind accompanying the rain. Suddenly, the lightbulb above burst into shards. He ducked and covered his head. While peeking around the corner, more lightbulbs shattered as though invisible bullets were shooting them. Each consecutive explosion made Patrick flinch.

"What the hell is going on?!" he yelled.

And when the interior returned to absolute darkness, a chill spread through the air. Patrick saw his breath in front of him. He pulled open one of the drawers and found a flashlight. Upon shining it, he realized that the entrance was open, allowing the water to flood the floors. He slogged through the aisles, making sure no one had entered the building.

As he reached the other end of the store, he spotted a white bedsheet something written on it: "OPEN THE TRUNK" in black ink. The bell above the door caught his attention and Patrick shined his flashlight at it.

"Who's there?" he called out. Footsteps stomped through the water, splashing and echoing through the store. Patrick peeked around the shelf and saw no one. Afterward, he returned his attention to the bedsheet, which was now a blank slate. He took in a deep breath and marched back to the counter, making sure to be fully aware of his surroundings. On his way there, he held the flashlight in a reverse grip, so he'd be ready to whack whatever lurked in the darkness.

"What the?"

He held his breath at the figure sitting on the floor behind the counter. His frail, skeletal body curled up to become as small as possible. As the water soaked through his jeans, he ignored the discomfort. He held his head low while his entire body shivered. At that moment, the figure's presence became overbearing. Patrick gently put one foot back behind him to step away, but the moment the heel of his shoe hit the water, a ripple effect spread across the surface.

"Why are you here?" the figure asked, defeatedly.

"Who are you?"

The boy slightly turned his face toward Patrick, and as his eye barely peeked through his long strands of hair, Patrick's heart fell. The boy was a spitting image of himself. A doppelgänger, with the only noticeable difference being his longer hair and younger appearance.

This can't be real.

"Who are you?!" Patrick yelled.

His other self turned his face away, burying his head between his knees.

"There's no good version of me, is there?"

Patrick stepped backward, still keeping the light aimed at the boy.

"Stop talking." He balled his hands into a tight fist.

"Sometimes, I tell myself it's been four years since Delan died and I'm only starting to heal. One time, I even convinced myself that I graduated from high school and university and became a prosecutor. But now, I see just how dangerous daydreaming can be. Tell me, how did you get here this time?"

Patrick tightly gripped the flashlight in one hand while he groped through the darkness for anything to use as a weapon. Eventually, he retrieved a mop, brandishing it in front of the figure.

"You better stay away."

"Always one to turn to violence. But it doesn't matter, I'm guilty of the same thing as well. Even she knows it."

Patrick's eyes narrowed on him.

"Who's she?"

"You haven't figured it out yet? Her name is Dabria. The woman who created this place." After uttering those words, his doppelgänger rotated to face the corner. He cried profusely into the palms of his hands. Patrick took slow strides toward him, intending to ask more questions.

"Promise me you won't give up on yourself," his clone pleaded.

In his confusion and anger, Patrick punched the corner of the counter, cutting his knuckles. A straight line of blood formed across his hand. Suddenly, a loud static surrounded him. He dropped everything he held to cover his ears before losing touch with reality.

???

MY JOURNAL

I can't do it. I can't be like him, and I can't handle Ms. Hawthorne. Every day, her advances get more extreme. First, she presses herself against me, and now she's taking my hand and putting it under her shirt. Is this really a fantasy I should love?

Chapter 15

PRESENT

The next thing Patrick knew, he was sitting in the chair with Luke by his side again. This time, no flood or any sign of destruction existed. Luke was still drawing in his sketchbook. He was working on a new image. One that depicted Sofia.

"What happened?" Patrick asked in a panic.

Luke flinched, appearing surprised to see him awake.

"Nothing. I was only drawing while you took a nap. See." He slid the drawing closer to Patrick. "I looked into Sofia's content a little more while you were out. The links she posts in each video brought me to a blog post. I read one about a woman. A really creepy one."

Patrick lay his trembling hands on the counter. His sweat soaked the smooth surface, making him feel sorry for Luke.

"I swear this store was flooded, and I saw someone who looked just like me."

He raised an eyebrow. "You probably had a nightmare."

"But it felt so real." Patrick looked down at his hands, noticing the cut he received from striking the counter was still present. He ran his finger along the red line, making sure that what he felt was real. "Show me all those things you found out about Sofia." Patrick said.

"Sure." Luke stuttered and rushed to get his phone as Patrick anxiously begged for his cooperation. After turning on his device, he handed it over. "You can sort through my tabs all you want."

"Thanks." Patrick viewed Sofia's first blog post, which was riddled with information regarding a woman in the small town of Twin Peaks. He zoomed in on each image, most of which contained sketches and old photographs of a lone woman in a blue dress. In some images, men in brown cloaks surrounded her; in others, she was alone. However, every depiction presented her as someone of high importance. And through it all, Sofia referred to the woman as Dabria.

This woman sees herself as some sort of angel who desires nothing more than to enact justice on those she deems 'guilty.' But her obsession with punishment makes her nothing more than an evil woman with a fascination for violence.

Patrick navigated further down the webpage, tapping each photo to make his own conclusions from it. After some time, he saw one image that piqued his interest. It was of a burnt brick wall.

While the picture itself didn't seem to have that much significance, he swore he recognized it. He thought back to his vacation with his family back in Skagway. A museum in the middle of the town held information regarding the entire state itself. While most of its history revolved around Skagway, a few pieces of information spoke of a town burned down in an accident.

Patrick felt a great sense of disappointment not being able to remember the ghost town, so he searched for archives of Skagway, hoping to find more information regarding the museum he visited.

"Is something wrong?" Luke asked.

Patrick brought his face back to a neutral demeanor as he realized how much he was scowling at his screen. "I swear, I've seen some of this town's history before."

Luke set down his pencil and slapped his backpack on the table.

"Let me handle it." He slid a laptop out of the front pocket of his carrier and waited for it to boot up. "Give me as much information as you can."

Luke smiled as he put his detective hat on, making Patrick realize how much interest he had in solving mysteries. The young man's big-toothed grin made his cheeks turn red, sending a shockwave through his heart. Patrick quickly clutched his chest as though his heart was ready to burst. He steadied his hands, reminding himself to push away the confusion he hadn't felt since his teenage years.

"Do you get heartburn or should I be worried it's something far more serious?" Luke rested his hand on his cellphone with the keypad ready. His finger twitched over the number nine until Patrick shook his head.

"No, just a bit of anxiety," he said.

Luke nodded, but his perplexed look didn't sit well with Patrick.

"Anyway, give me the details."

Patrick took in a deep breath as he dug into the inner recesses of his mind. "I saw it in a museum at the heart of the downtown area in Skagway. Of course, it mostly held pieces of Skagway's history, especially details about the gold rush. But at the back of the building was an exhibit about all of Alaska. That's where I saw a small slideshow of a town that burned down."

Luke leaned closer to his monitor. However, upon peeking, Patrick noticed his mouse cursor was still hovering over the search bar.

"What else?" Luke asked.

"Not much was known about the town, except that it was inland, a little closer to the Canadian border."

Luke nodded his head. "It's not much to go off, but I'm going to guess it's a pretty remote place and got burned down very early in the twentieth century."

Patrick raised an eyebrow. "What makes you say that?"

"We know almost nothing about the town, so it would make sense for the town to be quite secluded. That's why it had to have burned down way back when. If I remember correctly from my history classes, the U.S. were somewhat isolationist prior to World War Two. I wouldn't be surprised if hardly anyone knew one another."

"Wait, hold on. Americans weren't trying to isolate from each other, only from the war. At least until . . .you know what I mean."

Luke pursed his lips and waved his hand dismissively.

"I have nothing else to go on, anyway."

Patrick raised his eyebrow, wondering why Luke suddenly turned so brash.

"Yeah, but it's the only thing I can think of. Just give me some time to figure this out."

Patrick nodded and leaned back in his chair. While the heavy rain drenched everything it touched, the weather wasn't Patrick's biggest fear. Instead, the idea of being transported to another plane of reality lingered in his mind. He looked at the cut plaguing his knuckles.

Damn. He needed to know more. Was there any truth to Sofia's story and why was that boy sitting on the flooded floor a spitting image of him?

Chapter 16

PAST

Long after Patrick thought he had recovered from the mental scars left by the party, a patrol car drove into the parking lot. The sight of it made Patrick flinch. He jumped to his feet as though the vehicle itself were a horrid monster. However, the moment he turned on his heels, a familiar voice called out to him.

"Patrick!" it said.

Slowly, with fear gripping his heart, Patrick turned around, seeing Mr. Hawthorne glaring at him with his arms resting on top of his car door. He beckoned him to approach with a swift motion of his finger. So, when Patrick dragged his feet with his head hung low, Mr. Hawthorne sighed before stepping away and pointing at a red minivan parked behind him.

"You're lucky to have such a 'cool' teacher," he said.

Patrick lifted his head, seeing Ms. Hawthorne waving at him from her window. A strong sense of happiness made a smile form across his face, only to die at the sight of her frowning lips.

"I'll help my older sister any day. But be warned, even my loyalty to her has its limits," Mr. Hawthorne whispered in his ear.

"I understand," Patrick whispered.

Afterward, the officer slammed his door shut and drove away into the darkness of the night. Once Patrick entered the passenger seat, Ms. Hawthorne immediately started the ignition with no friendly banter. Only when they were a suitable distance away from the gas station did she open her mouth to speak.

"Honestly, I am upset with you. What you did tonight is stupid, but I'm not going to scold you until morning."

Patrick slumped his shoulders along with hers.

"Thank you and I'm sorry."

"There's no need to say sorry. Just promise me you won't do this again."

"I promise," Patrick said sadly.

Ms. Hawthorne rested her hand on his knee, giving him a warm smile.

"That's good. I know these past couple of days have been tough on you. That's why I'll give you a little gift."

Patrick cocked his head to the side, wondering what she was alluding to.

"I'll drive you back to my place. You can clean yourself up there."

"Is that the gift?"

Ms. Hawthorne giggled to herself. "No. It's much better. You'll see what I'm talking about."

Patrick forced a smile on his face, confused why the expression didn't come naturally to him. "Thank you," he mumbled.

Ms. Hawthorne gave him a quick side hug while brush her fingers against the back of his neck when she let him go. The touch of her skin made Patrick feel a mixture of fear, excitement, and confusion.

The same sensation of butterflies returned to his gut. Except this time, those butterflies felt more like insects escaping a ruthless predator. He had everything he could have wanted from Ms. Hawthorne. She supported him. She offered to keep him for a short period, and she was kind. So why didn't all of this sit well with him? Patrick held his hand over his abdomen and turned his face to the window, intending to hide the redness in his cheeks.

His emotions persisted well after they arrived at her house. On his way inside, Ms. Hawthorne ushered him up the stairs, toward her bedroom. "My bedroom has an attached shower. Just clean yourself up while I get you a towel and some clothes."

"Thank you." After she disappeared through the doorway, a quiet click reached his ears as he realized the lock on the knob had turned slightly. He gently pushed downward, coming face to face with the epiphany that Ms. Hawthorne had made him her own prisoner. Patrick pushed his negative feelings aside as he walked toward the bathroom.

I'll be naked. Of course, she doesn't want me wandering out. He repeated similar justifications in his head, but the warm lightbulbs filling the room with a red hue made his gut stir. He gulped hard as he placed his hand on the door to the bathroom. But just as soon as he did, he heard a shower head turn on downstairs. Patrick raised an eyebrow.

I thought this was the only bathroom? He faced the doorway before shaking his head.

He let out a deep breath, feeling silly for getting so scared. Perhaps he mistook the sound of the kitchen sink.

Without a second thought, he jumped into the shower and stood beneath the cascading water, letting it wash away the grime. He felt it clean his skin while he reveled in her soap and shampoo. For a moment, a smile spread across his face. The warm sensation spreading across his skin made him feel at home.

He looked at the shampoo, hoping to indulge in more, but his eyes locked onto an empty bottle next to it. He raised it to his face. Although the text had completely washed away, he could smell a fruity scent lingering around the cap. Suddenly, Ms. Hawthorne knocked on the door.

"I have some clothes at the door for you. I'll wait outside."

"Thank you!" Shortly after, he shut off the water and dried himself. Afterward, he peeked through the small opening he made when tugging on the knob. Ms. Hawthorne stood out of view, only making her back visible as she sat in front of her dresser. Patrick silently took the clothes and got ready to change.

However, he came to a quick stop looking at the familiar designs on the clothing. The shirt was black and depicted images from a music album that was popular among his male peers. Meanwhile, the pants fit him perfectly.

Whose clothes are these?

Patrick slipped into the clothes, realizing by the wrinkles that someone had worn them previously. He stamped out of the bathroom, thanking Ms. Hawthorne for her hospitality.

"Where are you going?" she asked in a bubbly tone. Patrick froze mid stride toward the exit.

"I'm sorry, but my parents are waiting for me at home and I'm tired."

"But what about your gift?" she asked, gesturing to the chair at the other end of her room.

"How about I pick it up tomorrow?"

Ms. Hawthorne took him by the hand, having to yank him away from the door. She placed him on the chair, standing over Patrick as he kept his attention on the carpet.

"You can't be serious? You're really going to make me wait?" she said, leaning toward his face. She pressed herself against him, forcing his face into her chest. He slightly pushed himself back, sinking deeper into the cushion.

Only then did the red glow bouncing off her walls haunt him. Soon, he saw the bedroom as more of a prison. Her beautiful portraits on the walls were merely propaganda, reinforcing an image of someone that didn't exist.

"Please, I have to go home," he whispered, barely able to get the words out of his throat. She lifted his hand and placed it slightly above her chest. Patrick retreated his limb, but she put a death grip on his wrist and clutched his hand. "Ms. Hawthorne, I have to go home now. My parents are waiting for me." A tear drop rolled down his cheek, to which she wiped it off his face with her finger. Afterward, she held his cheek with her hand.

"I know quite a bit about you. I see what you look at on social media. The way you ogle over your old babysitter. And just how much you want to be a 'man.'"

Patrick swallowed the lump that formed in his throat. He got up from the chair, pushed Ms. Hawthorne out of the way, and strode to the door. But after he turned the knob, he remembered the click from earlier. His ears followed Ms. Hawthorne's drunken-sounding laughter, and once his eyes rested on her, she slightly pulled down the top of her shirt, revealing the key dangling from her neck.

"It's inside my top," she whispered. Without hesitation, she wrapped her arms around Patrick's neck. In response, he shoved her, sending her to the floor. She sat still, rubbing her elbows that were red from carpet burn.

"Stay away from me!" he yelled.

"Listen! I didn't bring you over here just so you could get cold feet! I'm doing you a favor." She made sure to enhance her last sentence so that it sounded sweeter. Then she got closer to Patrick and placed his hand on her hips. "There's nothing wrong with this."

"There is," he said quietly.

"Listen, there are a lot of boys who'd love to be in your position. Isn't this a fantasy among you guys? The allure of an older and attractive woman? I see it a lot. Both in real life and in fiction. The films, the music and even some books." She ran her fingers over Patrick's chest, making him stagger. "You know, back when I was in college, we read Nabokov's work. Now what if we made a similar story?"

Patrick turned his head away. The butterflies in his stomach were now replaced by a blistering pain seeping into his heart.

"But . . . " His voice faded away while Ms. Hawthorne rested her forehead against his. "He didn't write 'Lolita' as a love story."

Ms. Hawthorne pressed her lips against his, and he held back the urge to vomit. When she finally retreated, she looked at him with bright eyes.

"Most students are afraid to correct their teachers. But you're not. You're a real man, you know that?" she hummed softly while resting her cheek on against Patrick's neck. "How about you just hold me and dance? Nothing else has to happen tonight. In fact, I'm sorry for comparing us to Nabokov's writing. What we have is so much more than that. It's love. Genuine love, not some horrible abomination."

Patrick quietly nodded his head, still feeling a great sense of discomfort. "Okay, but it's just a dance, right? And then I can go home?"

"Of course. I'd never hurt you," she whispered in his ear. After that, they gracefully waltz around the room while Patrick fought a war against his own mind.

Chapter 17

PRESENT

While Luke buried himself in his laptop, Patrick wandered through the aisles to stretch his legs. He passed the shelves, giving attention to absolutely nothing except for Luke. Occasionally, he'd look over his shoulder to watch him work and when his eyes weren't on him, the young man didn't escape his mind. Patrick fought himself, not knowing what to feel. Was he attracted to men or women? The hell it created for him ignited a riot in his brain. He couldn't deny the past. The time he spent with Ms. Hawthorne, his initial attraction to her, and how quickly that faded the night she took him to her house.

Am I bisexual? he asked himself. Patrick scoffed at the idea, pondering if maybe he was interested in women, but Ms. Hawthorne was the only exception. Patrick approached the exit, making a moment of eye contact with Luke.

"Don't hit your head again," he said.

Patrick nodded, put his hood up and walked toward the railing overlooking the cliff. Despite the inclement weather, the sight of the ocean combined with the forest reminded him of all the reasons he loved Alaska. He gave a faint smile and, as if on cue, the rain softened, turning from a heavy downpour to a slight drizzle. The clearing gave way for his eyes to adjust to the distance. The same mound of land that appeared earlier was closer than he expected.

"How many times have you wished for a different life?" a voice asked. Patrick turned around, seeing nothing but the empty parking lot. He turned back to the lake and gripped the railing. Looking down, the cut on his knuckles remained. "What life do you have this time?"

As more words spewed out of the entity's mouth, Patrick recognized it as his own. He fought hard to ignore it, but the more he resisted, the more determined it became.

"I wonder what Delan truly thinks of you."

"Stop talking," Patrick said through gritted teeth. As his willpower wavered, the rain quickly returned to its previous intensity. Suddenly, the weather was no longer on the verge of displaying clear skies. Instead, a storm brewed and as Patrick looked out at the water, even the waves began crashing on the rocks below.

"I'm real." the voice said.

"No, you're not."

"But we are."

"I said 'no'!" Patrick screamed. His cry bounced off the trees, shattering the silence of the nearby forest. Ravens flew through the sky as though his shrill voice plagued them with panic. He shut his eyes and took in a deep breath. Whoever this version of him was, it had to be nothing more than an entity preying upon him. At least, that's what he told himself. Patrick never shook off the feeling that he was being transported into the mysterious town Sofia spoke of in her videos.

He opened his eyes at the sudden sensation of fur rubbing against his freezing hands. Upon looking down, he saw Charlie nuzzling his nose against his cut knuckles.

"Hey there," Patrick said in a hushed tone. Charlie scratched the railing with his paw. Patrick stared at him, confused. But when he dismissed the dog's actions, Charlie threw away every ounce of subtly and ran under the railing.

"No!" Patrick leaned over the edge with his arm outstretched, but instead of seeing the animal falling down the cliff, he realized that he merely jumped to a ledge.

Patrick gazed down at the dirt-filled surface, realizing that Charlie was leading him somewhere. Resting next to his paws were footprints, along with an open matchbox and other camping supplies.

Patrick looked over his shoulder, through the gas station windows. Instead of going back to purchase tools and make a safe descent, he figured it'd be best to leave Luke to investigate the town. Otherwise, buying rope would distract the man by starting a conversation about why Patrick needed such equipment.

After rubbing his hands together, he threw one leg over the rails and gently set his foot down on the first rock he felt. With steady movements, he gradually made his way downward until he arrived at the ledge where Charlie waited.

The dog looked toward an empty cave while Patrick stared onward in astonishment.

Was this here the whole time?

A gust of wind escaped the dark cavern and halted. Patrick sorted through the matchbox, finding a single good match.

Without further preparations, he followed Charlie into the crevice in the Earth. The sound of the rain disappeared when Patrick delved into the cave. Once all traces of light vanished, he struck the match, offering a small glimmer of hope within the darkness.

Charlie's paws pattered against the small puddles of water littering the ground. Meanwhile, Patrick smelled the scent of the ocean lingering under his nose. He pushed forward, finally pausing when piles of heavy stones blocked his path.

He sighed, disappointed at the obstacle. Upon closer inspection, he saw a small hole in between the rocks. While the crevice wasn't large enough to move through, he pressed his eye against it. Noticing a teenage boy cowering on the floor, Patrick lifted the match up, warming the right side of his face. The boy had long dark hair, just as he did. Except his black locks reached the floor and covered his entire body.

"Who are you?" Patrick asked. The kid turned his head, peeking at Patrick through the small slits in his curls. The boy sighed and buried his head in between his knees.

"Oh, it's you again," the boy said.

Patrick narrowed his eyes at him.

"What are you talking about?" He pushed his chest closer to the hole, trying to get as close as possible.

"Just go away. Haven't you done enough damage?"

Patrick pursed his lips. While the teen's words sent confusion running through his body, the ghastly sight of him made Patrick feel sad more than anything else. The kid was vulnerable, resembling Delan in the last days he was alive.

"I've been seeing things. I'm trying to find out what's going on." Patrick's voice trembled as he grew more desperate to understand these apparitions. "Do you know what I mean?" Patrick raised his volume while pressing his hands further into the stones.

"Yes," the boy said bluntly.

Patrick gently poked his match through the tiny opening to get a good look at the stranger. He realized that under the boy's long hair, he was almost naked. Only the dirty boxers he wore kept him from being completely exposed.

"I can help you. I'll get you out of there. All you have to do is talk to me."

The kid stood tall and turned around. Patrick's chest tightened after seeing his facial features. It was another doppelgänger. Another imposter pretending to be him. But rather than showing hostility, he sought the path of empathy, deciding that compassion would give him a far better chance at getting the information he wanted.

"Good. You're doing good. If you could come forward and-"

The kid dashed forward, turning himself into a blur, and by the time he became visible, he pressed his face against the narrow opening. He made eye contact with Patrick as he forced his fingers through the gaps. His coarse skin trembled over Patrick's as though he were the first human he had come across in centuries.

"How'd you get here?" His other self asked.

"I climbed down the cliff."

The other version of himself shook his head. "No, I mean, what brought you to this place? What's your life like?"

Patrick frowned. "Four years ago, Delan died. I'm here to get away from the world. To just relax while I have a vacation in Skagway."

"Skagway? I remember that place. You're the first one of us to come here besides me."

Patrick bit on the inside of his cheek. "Who's 'us'? Are there more of you who look like me?"

The boy slowly backed away and Patrick fought the urge to reach out in a futile attempt to touch him. "We are you," his doppelgänger said ominously.

"Listen, I need some answers. Not this cryptic bullshit! Tell me what's going on! Why am I seeing things? What is this place, and why do you look like me?"

Rather than answering one of his questions, his other self faced the rocky ground before choosing to sulk in the corner.

"You can break the cycle. All you have to do is find the courage to face the truth."

Patrick's breath turned heavy as the frustration stirring within him grew into an unbearable anger.

"That's doesn't answer my questions!" he yelled. After his sudden outburst, a short pause enveloped them both, only for a gust of wind to enter the cavern and snuff out the match.

Patrick heard the air sweeping through the cracks between the stones, followed by the sound of bare feet sprinting over shallow puddles.

"Please, break this cycle," his doppelgänger whispered. A pair of lips brushed against Patrick's ear and soon a match struck in front of him.

As the flame illuminated his surroundings, Patrick realized the rocks were no longer there. Instead, his clone stood in front of him, holding his own match to cast away the darkness. He dangled an emerald brooch in front of his eyes. It swung from side to side like a pendulum and Patrick's pupils followed it.

"Sofia's words are true. That town is real. You're not in Skagway. You never have been. You were always in--"

The name of the town drifted away, silencing every syllable.

"What was that?" Patrick asked.

His doppelgänger shook his head in disappointment.

"Here. Find a woman named Dabria. This belonged to her." He laid the brooch in Patrick's hand before looking him in the eyes. "I wish I could tell you everything, but it's imperative that you find the truth and accept it of your own accord. Otherwise, you'll never be able to break this cycle."

"Wait!" Patrick called to him, but the match had already been put out. Suddenly, the cave rumbled, sending down pieces of rocks from the ceiling.

"Charlie!" The dog finally whirred to life after sitting calmly for so long. He ran down the path they entered, barking along the way. Patrick followed him toward the light of the outside world. He leapt forward, landing just at the edge of the cliff.

"Thank you." He petted Charlie as he caught his breath. Afterward, he shoved the brooch into his pocket and began ascending the cliff.

Chapter 18

PRESENT

By the time Patrick grabbed the railing, the mud covered his chest, and enough dirt clung to his fingernails to grow a garden. However, despite the exhausting experience, he didn't waste any time in pulling himself over the metal bars and sprinting toward the gas station. He barged through the door, realizing that the place was empty.

"Luke?" Patrick called out, but received no response.

Charlie trotted inside and vigorously shook himself dry. Once the door shut, Charlie ran around the counter and used his front paws to raise himself up on its surface. He barked at the laptop screen.

"What have you got there?" Patrick made his way toward Charlie, expecting to see something paranormal. The screen read: *Welcome to Twin Peaks.* Suddenly, the monitor flickered on and off until it settled on the image of two spiraling towers, reaching endlessly into the sky. A muffled sound came from the laptop. Patrick brushed Charlie aside as he pressed the button to raise the volume.

"Twin Peaks, that's where my characters went," Sofia's voice spoke. "It's a place where people go after committing sins. It plays with them. It turns things that were familiar into something horrific. Worst of all, no one knows when they're transported into this 'otherworld' until it's too late."

Quickly, the laptop shut off, leaving Patrick alone with nothing but the heavy rain to listen to. He walked toward the break room, hoping that Luke hadn't disappeared. That there was something he could make sense of. But when he opened the door, he found nothing except for a blank book.

"Charlie!" Patrick called for the dog, who was scrounging behind the counter. He heard Charlie ripping through various bags as though some treasure were hidden inside. "Get over here."

Patrick sighed and turned on his heels, wishing Charlie would linger next to him rather than appearing and disappearing. But before he made any distance, the brooch in his pocket pulled him back. He felt the force of the jewelry tugging at his jeans. He grunted as he stomped his feet into the ground to keep himself from falling, but soon emerald colors shined in his eyes as the object flew out of his pocket and onto the book.

Patrick watched it sink into the blank page, slowly turning into a black-and-white image. Then a breeze brushed against his skin. The pages that were once blank now bled with black ink, turning it from a blank canvas into an entire story. Patrick took one step forward, only for the door behind him to swing shut.

"No!" he yelled. He gripped the handle and pulled tight, but to no avail. It was stuck in place, refusing to budge.

"Read it!" a woman's voice commanded. Patrick gritted his teeth, recognizing her as one of the people he heard earlier.

Reluctantly, he turned around to face the terrible sight. Black ink now covered the white table where the book lay. It spread over the surface like a running river. But on the pages was a detailed description of the year Delan passed away. The reminders of his neglect of his brother, fueled by his insecurities, littered the pages.

"Stop!" Patrick yelled. He fell to his knees, covering his face as he coward from the sight. And soon, the pages couldn't hold the ink anymore as the book became drenched in black liquid. The ink converged at the edge of the table, forming one large clump that hit the ground, turning into a giant splash, and from that stain, a woman slowly rose.

Patrick crawled backward and pressed himself against the door. He looked up, terrified at the sight. "Who are you?" he asked sheepishly.

As the ink slowly formed the body of the woman, her dark form turned to color. Shades of blue rose from the ebony liquid until her dress fully formed. After the dress emerged, the woman's hands turned into a light skin tone, followed by her face, and soon, her brown hair appeared. The woman took in a deep breath as she opened her eyes.

She gradually looked down, keeping her attention on Patrick. Half of her face held red streaks across them while the bits and pieces of her skin remained burned.

"Hello, Patrick. My name is Dabria." The woman spoke plainly, and Patrick stared at her without saying a word. "You've given me the same look four times now."

"I. . ." Patrick gulped hard. Sweat formed around his wrist as he pulled his knees closer to his chest.

"Do you know what brought you to this place? Why you're here?"

"Because I let my brother down," he muttered.

Dabria shook her head. "It is true, you disappointed Delan greatly, but there was something else you did to be brought here."

Patrick shuddered and hugged himself. "I don't know," he whispered.

"Well, you better think, because not a single person brought into this realm is innocent."

Patrick quickly glanced over his shoulder at the door.

"Luke! Charlie!"

Dabria sighed.

"Don't call for Luke. The young man couldn't even act like a real person. It's a shame. I sent the boy here to guide you, but it appears he wasn't suitable for the job. And that dog. What a pain he's been."

Patrick slowly got to his feet with wobbling legs.

"Let me go." he begged.

Dabria frowned.

"I can only let you go when you've accepted the truth on your own terms."

She sighed and looked at the floor. "Perhaps those apparitions born of your own guilt will help you. I know you see me as a monster. Everyone does but know this. I want to see you succeed. I want to see you acknowledge your wrongdoing and become a better man." After that, her whole body turned into black ink, and she disappeared into the pages.

Chapter 19

PAST

Ms. Hawthorne pressed her forehead against his while Patrick awkwardly maneuvered his sweaty palms around her waist. His throat tightened with disgust, but he felt conflicted. In a sense, she was right that he always wanted a partner, but he'd never guess that this was the situation he'd find himself in.

"Listen, Ms. Hawthorne . . . "

She grinned at him and closed her eyes. A surge of anxiety shot throughout his body, pouring out his skin in copious amounts of sweat.

She closed her eyes? A kiss? Patrick shut his own eyes, fearing that she'd take things a step further, but he heard her humming a tune.

"You're pretty good at this," she whispered.

Patrick opened his eyes, realizing that she had been staring at him. She placed her palm on his cheek, and he pulled back. With his head creating some distance, he finally felt like he had some room to breathe. "I'm sorry."

Ms. Hawthorne chuckled. "You look cute when you're flustered."

"Ms. Hawthorne, can I go home now?"

She lay her head on his chest. "You can call me Jasmine. All my friends do."

"Okay . . .Ms--I mean Jasmine. Can I go home?"

"What's the matter?" She pressed herself against him and ran her fingers through his hair. Her eyes caught his attention, as she fawned over him like a teenager in a drama film.

"This is wrong. This is so wrong." Patrick let go of her and tip toed backward. Ms. Hawthorne stood still with her hands on her hips.

"Well, this is disappointing," she said harshly.

"Look, I have to go."

"What about your brother? What about Delan?"

Patrick stood still, eyeing her every move. From the way she spread her lips to the glint of her tooth in the dim lamplight, he stared at her, wondering why she brought his sibling up now. "What about him?"

"I'm a teacher. Imagine how many students I see and talk to daily. Think of all the information I can give you. Not only that, but you already know who my brother is."

Patrick scoffed at her. "So what?"

"Simple. I just want you to open up to me. You don't need to be so guarded." She closed the distance within a second and pinched his cheeks as though she were his mother. "You're safe here. You can come to me for anything." She embraced him, squeezing him to where he could hardly breathe. Yet, despite her display of affection, Patrick could only let out a teardrop.

"Thank you," he said dispassionately.

"You're welcome." She gave him a light peck on the cheek before opening the door. I'll drive you home. Don't worry about your car. My brother and I will take care of it."

Patrick quietly nodded his head and followed her outside like he was a captive and she was a soldier with a rifle aimed at his back. And after he entered her vehicle, he zoned out for the rest of the night.

"Here you go," she said. By now, they had parked in front of his house. An orange hue painted the clouds as the sun gently pierced through. Ms. Hawthorne leaned closer to Patrick with her lips puckered out, but when the curtain inside his living room swiftly moved, she retreated. Though disappointment showed on her face, Patrick felt grateful, as though he had just been saved. He quickly left her car without saying a goodbye and entered his abode.

"Where the hell have you been?" his dad asked angrily. He pointed to the clock hanging above the mantel of the fireplace. The hands ticked slowly, revealing that it was well past midnight. "Do you have any idea how worried your mother was? Why didn't you answer your phone? At the very least, you could have sent us a text message!"

Patrick lowered his gaze. "Dad, I'm sorry."

"Don't apologize to me. Apologize to your mom!"

"Why should I? You know how controlling she is! Hell, I—"

"Don't talk about her like that!" His voice boomed throughout the house. Fear ran through Patrick's body. His eyes darted toward his parent's bedroom door, expecting his mother to burst out and send a hailstorm of her angry scolding. "Luckily for you, she's cried herself to sleep by now. I sure hope that girl was worth all this trouble." His voice trailed off.

"Girl?"

"Don't play dumb with me. I saw her leaning in for that kiss. And why the tainted windows? You don't want us to see her?"

Patrick tightly gripped the pillow on the couch as he sat down, trying to contain his anger. "Dad, it's not a big deal. Weren't you happy for me, anyway?"

"Yes, I was, but not anymore. Listen, I know you're stressed because of Delan, but that's no excuse to disappear for an entire night. Your mother thought you went and killed yourself as well. We even called the cops. The same officer, Mr. Hawthorne, came by again. He said he'd handle it. And judging by the way you came back, I suppose someone else did his job for him."

His dad slammed his fist into the coffee table. After which, a pang of guilt struck his face. He slowly raised his trembling palm, staring into it like it was an empty abyss. A deep exhale escaped the man's chest.

"I'm sorry," Patrick muttered under his breath. He swore he noticed a tiny teardrop form around the corner of his father's eye, but just before it could roll down his cheek, he whipped his face in the opposite direction.

"You know, my girlfriend has been helping me through this," he lied. Patrick's throat tightened when he referred to Ms. Hawthorne as his 'girlfriend.' Despite the fear she instilled in him, he didn't know what else to refer to her as.

"You don't have to tell your mother and I about everything. But at the very least, let her know you're safe."

"What's this about Mom? Don't you hate her tantrums too?"

His dad stomped around the room as though resisting the urge to break something. "Of course I do, but you don't know her like I do. Yes, she can be overbearing. Yes, she gets angry. But deep down, she still loves you!"

Patrick averted his gaze. This time, his dad couldn't hold back his tears. "I-I'm sorry. I don't want to yell at you, but what you've done is just too... Too careless," he finally said. While Patrick couldn't let go of the way his mother treated him, he couldn't deny the good she's done. From the long hours she spent at work to the times she watched over him when his father couldn't. Her presence had the occasional touch of warmth, despite her imperfections.

"Just go to your room. You better wake up by noon to hug your mom."

Patrick stood from the couch with shame shackling his feet to the floor.

"Yes." He spoke in a whisper.

From then on, he had to use all his might to drag his feet upstairs. The guilt, combined with his father's sadness, put a spell on him. A strong type of magic that made him want to fall into a deep sleep to avoid any sort of responsibility. And when he finally lay in bed, he thought back to his dance, feeling more frustrated with his feelings toward Mrs. Hawthorne. By now, the anger, fear and disgust left him, making way for confusion to fill his heart.

If this is every boy's fantasy, why am I living in a nightmare?

Chapter 20

PRESENT

After Dabria left, Patrick quickly opened the door, only to realize he was alone in the station. He walked through the aisles, searching for Charlie, who seemed to have disappeared once again.

Patrick grunted and turned to the window to look outside. The rain consumed everything, creating a massive flood. As the world became drenched, fog stained the glass, cutting off his view of the outside world. Patrick let out a deep breath as the cold seeped through the cracks of the door. And as he stood still, staring into the fog, he saw his brother's reflection. Patrick stifled a gasp.

"What are you?" he asked.

A frown formed on Delan's face.

"Do you really need to ask that?"

Patrick sucked in a deep breath. He could feel his emotions bubbling to the surface, wanting to break through his stone-cold face.

"Are you a ghost?"

"No."

"Are you something in my head?"

"No."

In the glass, Delan's arms wrapped around his shoulders and Patrick shut his eyes as he felt his little brother's embrace. He thought of turning around, but he remembered the interactions he had in his car. What if he glanced over his shoulder only for Delan to disappear? What if Delan's reflection was the only way he could see him?

"I'm sorry," Patrick stammered. "I can't take back what I did to you. How much I let you down."

"Don't cry, please," Delan begged him.

"I can't. I can't stop." Patrick's breath turned into a small cloud hovering in front of his lips. He thought back to his high school years. The stress he put on his parents haunted him. He remembered the morning Ms. Hawthorne drove him home and the argument he had with his father.

"I got too caught up in finding your 'girlfriend' even though the answer was right in front of me. I let my warped view of masculinity separate me from you." Patrick sniffled as he cried. "I'm sorry. For everything."

Delan hugged him tighter. "There's more to it."

"What do you mean?" Patrick asked.

"If I told you myself, you wouldn't believe it. You wouldn't break the cycle."

Patrick clenched his fist and shut his eyes. He tried to retrace his steps. From the beginning of that school year until the day it ended, he saw his brother as a cheerful boy, exploring the campus. Then he noticed the sadness that slowly etched itself into his face as the year went on. The argument they had when Patrick picked him up after detention. To the night he tried to stab himself. But as he delved deeper into his memories, his legs grew weak. They wobbled as though every single muscle lost power.

"All I see is the neglect I showed you. The stupid things I did to act like a 'real man.'" Patrick opened his eyes and saw Delan staring back at him with a blank expression.

"Patrick, you're so close. Keep searching."

"B-but I don't know what you're talking about. I wasn't a good brother. Isn't that the terrible sin I've committed?"

Delan shook his head.

"There's more to it, and you already know the truth. You've just shut it away."

"I don't know what you're talking about!' Patrick cried profusely. "I just know I treated you terribly. That's why I'm here! Stop torturing me, please. Am I really supposed to break some sort of cycle, or is that just talk to put me into some never-ending chase for something I won't find?"

Delan's eyes lowered to the floor. He tightened his arms around Patrick's shoulders.

"I wouldn't lie to you."

And with that, a small bit of blood seeped from Delan's forehead, right below his hairline. Patrick looked helplessly at the reflection. Soon, the tiny red droplet grew into a long line, streaking down his face.

"No!" Patrick screamed. Delan's arms loosened. Patrick knew his brother was going to disappear once more.

The blood drenched Delan's face, turning him into nothing more than a fountain of red. Delan closed his eyes, letting himself turn into mush. The wetness of his blood spread to Patrick, leaving behind red stains on his coat. Like a lit candle, Delan melted into a red pool at Patrick's feet. The puddle he left behind gradually formed a smooth rectangle. It slowly turned solid until it became a book. Patrick picked it up, realizing it was Delan's old journal. The journal revealed multiple entries of his brother's deepest secrets to him, but as he flipped through the pages, he realized the depth of his actions' impact on Delan.

He strode toward the counter, clutching the leatherbound book in his hands. The chair groaned as Patrick sat. With his head staring at the smooth surface, he carefully placed the journal down and read.

"I can't take it anymore. All Patrick does is sit at his stupid desk playing his stupid games. I hate him. Maybe if I tell him that real men don't play games. That they work and make money, then he'll leave his room. But of course, it'll only be because he cares about his image. Why can't he see that I want him to be himself? The same way I always remembered him?

"Each day, I go to school, and each day, I get detention. The curtains stay shut so Ms. Hawthorne can have her way with me. Even after the entire ordeal ends, I still feel her fingers caressing my neck. I can still feel her breath on my skin. The way her lips feel against mine. It's so disgusting. If I could, I'd tell Patrick all about it, but what if he laughs? What if he tells me I'm lucky? I just want my brother.

"Tonight. I'm going out again. She's so persistent. Maybe, if I give her what she wants, she'll let me go, and I should be able to get to her with no problems. Mom and Dad are asleep and Patrick is shut inside his room again. I don't even have to sneak out. It's not like I have to hide from them.

Patrick took a deep breath as his fingers lifted the corner of the page. He went to the next section, where only one sentence remained.

She raped me, it read. Patrick buried his face in his hands.

"He needed me and I let him down," he whispered to himself. He stared out the window once more, seeing another doppelgänger approaching the store. This time, he looked older. A little more rugged with a fully grown beard and a cigarette in his mouth. Patrick tapped his fingers against the counter as he waited patiently.

Think. What am I missing about the past? What is it?

The man stepped inside the store and flicked his cigarette behind him. As his heavy boots echoed across the floor, Patrick brought his eyes up to meet his own.

"Another me," Patrick said bluntly.

The man nodded. He straightened his suit and took his hat off.

"Let's have a chat, shall we?"

Patrick didn't say a word. He simply accepted everything that took place. The transition he experienced from the gas station to this paranormal realm happened so fast he couldn't grasp it.

"I never thought I'd find myself in Twin Peaks like this," Patrick muttered.

"I think you already know that –"

"That I was always here," Patrick finished his sentence. The man grinned, rested his elbows on the counter, and leaned forward.

"In my life, I began my career as a police officer and eventually became a detective. My hate toward pedophiles brought me to so many cases regarding missing and abused children. I made up a brand new identity for myself. One that persisted well into my forties. But I guess that's what happens when the truth hurts so much."

Patrick's back stiffened as he stared into the eyes of the man in front of him. He had the beard. He had the cigarette, and he had the gruff voice Patrick always wanted.

"And?"

"Well, it was a lie. I was in Seattle investigating the case of a missing girl, and then everything slowly changed. Things felt odd. Nothing seemed real, and that's when I met her. Dabria."

Patrick nodded, only to acknowledge what he said.

"You've already met the others, haven't you?"

"Yes," Patrick said slowly.

The man whistled a soft tune before bringing his attention to the trunk of Patrick's car.

"You're the fourth one to come here .and hopefully the last," the man said without turning around. "I know you smelled the scent ruminating in your vehicle. I smelled it in mine, but when I opened it, I refused to believe it. Hopefully, whatever is inside will remind you of what really happened."

Patrick looked toward his car. From out of the bushes, Charlie appeared, holding a crowbar in his mouth. Patrick's doppelgänger gave a slight chuckle.

"That little guy tried to guide me too, just like everyone else. I'm sure it pains him to see you still struggling."

Patrick got off his chair and stared at his car.

"Let me ask you something."

"Anything."

Patrick thought for a minute to arrange his words properly.

"Are you like Luke? The guy was someone Dabria sent to watch over me."

His doppelgänger shook his head.

"No. Twin Peaks has always made monsters like me to represent the deepest fears of each person who came here."

"But you don't look like a monster," Patrick said, confused.

"Monsters aren't always scary creatures. Sometimes, they look like people, and sometimes, they're something we hold in that scares us."

Patrick raised his eyebrows. "I don't get it."

The man patted his shoulder. "I'm sorry for rambling."

Patrick nodded his head. "Why do you all look like me?"

His doppelgänger walked toward the exit without answering him. As soon as he opened the door, he peered over his shoulder, making eye contact with Patrick.

"Be honest. Do you see yourself as a monster?"

Chapter 21

PAST

As soon as the morning sun struck Patrick's face, he rolled out of bed. When he left his room, he peeked his head over the stairway to see if his mother was already awake. However, the first floor of the house remained completely vacant, save for the unfinished dishes left on the dining table.

Patrick carefully mounted the steps, hoping to not to wake his parents to buy enough time to calm his nerves. But as soon as he reached the first floor, he found his mom's cellphone lying on the kitchen table next to a note that read *call us.* Patrick quickly took the mobile device, turned it on, and shuffled through his mother's contact list.

The moment he began the call with his father; he rested the device against the side of his face, praying that nothing horrible had surfaced.

"Patrick!" his dad said, sounding panicked. In the background, he heard his mother crying out in anguish. A certain type of sobbing that he never expected to hear.

"What's wrong?" he asked, confused.

His father took a deep breath before speaking. "It's Delan. We got a call that he threatened to hurt himself again, so they held him in a different ward."

Patrick held the cellphone in a death grip. "Okay, but it's just a threat, right? Even if he meant to hurt himself, they stopped him, right?" Each word made it more apparent how desperate he sounded. Images of the night when Delan held the knife haunted him. "Right?" he spoke louder.

"Yes, they stopped him," his father said. "But we probably won't hear from him for a while. He's refusing to take anymore phone calls or visits."

Patrick swallowed the lump that formed in his throat. Whoever was with Delan that night had to pay. "Alright, did he do anything else, say anything else?"

"I really don't know, but your mother and I will be here until we find out what we can." Afterward, his dad hung up the phone. Patrick paced the kitchen, wondering what he should do first. He knew that school started within an hour and while he dreaded his classes, he still had to find Delan's mysterious girlfriend. But before that, he went to his brother's bedroom to search for anything that proved to be useful. Whether it be a secret journal, some clothes that still lingered with the smell of perfume or even something as miniscule as an out of place cup.

He began at his brother's dresser. His fingers dug through every single one of Delan's clothes. Patrick occasionally sniffed the air in front of him to see if the perfume was still present and, much to his amazement, it wasn't.

He searched Delan's desk, rummaging through each drawer and examining every paper inside. Most of the materials he found were overdue pieces of homework, but one thing that caught Patrick's eye was a blank notebook.

Patrick picked it up and stared at it curiously. Delan usually organized everything he owned, so why was this item not labeled? Without further questions, Patrick dug into the spiral-bound notebook.

At first glance, he merely saw paragraphs upon paragraphs of dated entries. When the realization that it was a journal hit him, a smile spread across Patrick's face. It soon faded when he noticed the dates were all from years ago and came to an abrupt stop when Delan entered high school.

Patrick uttered a cuss, feeling pained at the disappointing revelation that the journal would not offer anything recent. He sighed and put the item back in its place, only for a small polaroid picture to escape from it. It slowly fluttered downward onto the carpet. Patrick gently retrieved it.

His eyes opened wide when he saw it was a relatively new picture. Although Delan looked slightly younger, judging by the background, Patrick knew the photo was taken this year.

Feeling somewhat giddy at his luck for stumbling upon a new piece of evidence, he laid it on the desk and hunched over to examine the image. He saw that Delan's face still held a smile, but his eyes fixated on something else. The faint reflection of a woman in the clock above the wall told Patrick that Delan was staring at someone. And then, he slammed his fist on the desk at the epiphany that it was the same woman he saw the night his brother came home. Her outline was unmistakable. However, since he could only see her hair color, it didn't give him much more information to work with.

While her face wasn't clear, Patrick knew that the woman's unique hairstyle would be enough to pin-point her. It was dyed black with streaks of red. Surely, such a look would stick out to him, but no one at school had dyed hair like that.

Patrick pursed his lips and scoured the picture for more information. He eventually concluded that since it appeared to be taken at the beginning of the school year, the girl probably dyed her hair at that point in time and let the colors slowly fade. All he had to do was ask around to find out who had an eccentric sense of fashion six months ago.

Patrick carried the photo to his bedroom and rested it on his desk, where he thought it would be safe. Afterward, he dialed Ms. Hawthorne's phone number.

"Who is this?" she asked, answering his call.

"Hey, this is Patrick. I'm using my mom's phone, but don't worry, I'll delete the call history afterward."

Ms. Hawthorne hummed in agreement.

"It's best we don't use your mom's phone at all. You can search for me on social media and send a message."

"Fine, but how about—" Before he could finish, she hung up. Patrick sighed, deleted the contact history, and slapped the phone face-down on the desk. With a short grumble escaping his throat, he turned on his computer to find Ms. Hawthorne's profile. After scrolling through the faces of many women, Patrick finally found her and sent her a message.

It's me, Patrick.

He tapped his fingers impatiently over his hardened desk as three dots appeared on the screen, showing she was in the middle of typing a message.

Don't send a friend request. Otherwise, what do you need?

I need to see you as soon as I get to school.

Patrick waited for her to respond. However, when two minutes passed, he sent another message.

Are you still there?

Yes. How about you meet me at my house?

No, I found a lead to find the one responsible for this mess. I need to get this person.

Patrick leaned back in his chair and fidgeted with the photograph. He eyed the girl one more time, wishing that he could pick her out from everyone else.

Just meet me at my house first.

No, I need to get to school. After firmly stating his stance, Patrick stood from his chair and walked to the other end of the room to retrieve his school bag. Not long after picking it up, he heard a notification echo through his speakers.

On the screen, Ms. Hawthorne had sent a photograph along with the image of a kissing face. Standing there in the nude, Ms. Hawthorne struck a pose with the caption: *I'm waiting for you.* Patrick grimaced at the sight before hovering his fingers over the keys.

Listen, I really need to figure this out first. He clutched his chest, knowing that for Delan's sake, he had to remain focused.

If you don't come here, I won't help you.

Patrick slammed his fist down onto his desk. *Fine.*

He marched out of his room and down the stairwell, stopping at the fridge first. He yanked it open, only to be greeted by the cool gust of air striking his cheeks. His father's beer bottles shined within the light like an old friend. Patrick gave them a long stare before deciding that he may as well try one out, hoping it would calm his nerves. At least then, he'd be able to face Ms. Hawthorne to abide by the rules she set out for him. Patrick took a tiny sip before gagging and bringing it with him to his car.

After flooring the gas pedal downward, he sped to Ms. Hawthorne's residence, feeling only dread. He looked into the rearview mirror, wishing that Delan were there to speak to him. While he waited at a traffic light, Patrick pulled down the sun visor to reveal the picture hidden inside. In the photo, Delan was a little boy, smiling at the camera.

I'll fix this. Patrick whispered to him. The moment the light turned green; it was a straight path toward Ms. Hawthorne's house.

At his arrival, she immediately opened the door, already in a robe, which Patrick assumed bore nothing but her exposed body underneath. He brought his adult beverages with him and sat on the coach, zoning out as he let Ms. Hawthorne do as she wished. By the end of the ordeal, he felt dirty, as though he was a pig crawling through the mud. While he lay on the couch, half naked, Ms. Hawthorne ran her fingers through his hair.

"How was it?" she asked.

"Good," Patrick said flatly.

His teacher grinned at him and ran her finger across his lips. "Just 'good'?"

"Yes." Patrick closed his eyes and took in a deep breath. *This doesn't feel right.*

"I've never seen you with a girl. Was I your first?"

At her question, Patrick stood tall and made a beeline toward the kitchen. He washed his face, getting as much of his skin as possible. While Ms. Hawthorne stared at him, dumbfounded, Patrick held back the urge to cry. At some point, something such as this would have been his fantasy. The allure of being with an attractive woman, regardless of the age difference, seemed like a deal leaning his favor, so he hid his trembling hands beneath the running water as though he could hide it from himself.

"Didn't you like it?" she asked him.

Patrick gargled water in his mouth and spit it out before answering her. "No, you were great." With one clean flick of his wrist, he shut off the tap. Her voice grated on his ears, and he doubted he could keep himself together. After what transpired on the sofa, the thought of lingering in her house felt like the death penalty. "Now, you can help me, right?"

"Haven't I already helped you?" Her cheeks flushed red, and she giggled with her finger pointed at him.

"I meant a different kind of help. I found something that could help me track down the girl responsible for hurting Delan."

He walked toward her with the photograph in hand. Her eyes followed it as it made a soft landing on the coffee table.

"See this?" Patrick stabbed his finger into the faint reflection of the dyed hair. "You see hundreds of students every day. Do you know who this girl is?"

A long paused enveloped them both. "I-I'm not sure."

Patrick slumped his back, looking defeated. "Please, give me something to work with."

Ms. Hawthorne rested her chin on his shoulder while staring at the photograph. Her soft breathing lingered on the skin of his neck, striking fear in his heart. "I truly don't know. You kids always express yourself in odd ways."

Patrick pursed his lips, hating himself for not having the courage to spit in her face. "Really? Nothing at all?"

"Nope. Absolutely nothing."

Patrick slumped his shoulders, buried his face inside his palms. The knowledge of his brother's mental torment made stress stir within him. Ms. Hawthorne noted his shakiness and placed her hand on his.

"Did something happen to Delan?" she asked in a whisper.

"Yes, he threatened to take his life again."

Ms. Hawthorne embraced him, resting her face on his chest. Patrick gave her a slight nudge to give himself room to breathe.

"I can cheer you up. All it takes is another round with me."

Patrick averted her gaze, but she clasped his face, only to turn his attention back to her. He tensed his neck to fight against her advances, but in the end, he gave in. "That's it. This is what boys your age want."

Patrick squirmed, looking for the courage to tell her 'no.' Yet no matter how much he wanted to break away, he still thought of the pressure he felt to fit in.

This hurts. It hurts so much. He tried to imagine Ms. Hawthorne wearing a bag over her head to avoid looking at the woman who was taking advantage of him, but it didn't work, and his need to be like 'Khen' and his peers with vastly more experience than him, only made the pain worse.

Once their eyes met, he realized that the woman he once knew was never there to begin with. Instead, a mere creature born of pure malice had been center stage, and now he felt stuck.

"Okay," he said quietly. While she nuzzled him down onto the couch, Patrick hated her for what she was doing and he hated himself for putting sexual experiences on a pedestal.

Chapter 22

PRESENT

After his last doppelgänger left the store, Patrick stood, motionless. *Am I a monster?* He thought to himself. He slowly raised his hands, viewing his palms from the back and the front. The question made his fingers shake. With a heavy breath, he gritted his teeth, holding back the urge to scream. He walked around the counter and stared into the parking lot right at his vehicle. The trunk waited for him, its back lights flashing like a massive beacon. He pressed his nose to the glass and closed his eyes. He tuned in to the sound of the rain, imagining himself back in Iowa.

One night, he and Delan snuck out of the house after watching a video of some men driving through a storm. The way those cameras chased down tornadoes despite the danger stirred something within them. Perhaps Patrick was jealous of their bravery, while Delan just wanted to have an adventure with his older brother. Patrick clenched and unclenched his fist. The moisture left behind by his sweat rivaled the poignancy of the rain.

And before he could leave the station, the bell above the door rang. He peeked around the shelves, expecting to see another doppelgänger or even Dabria. But instead, Charlie waited for him with a crowbar held tightly in his mouth. He tilted his head forward and dropped the tool. This time, his tail didn't wag, and he didn't shake his body to dry his thick coat. Instead, he waited there like a statue.

"Thanks," Patrick said. He walked forward and bent over to pick up the crowbar. Like a loaded rifle, the heavy metal tool felt significant in his hands. He examined it, noticing a white piece of tape barely hanging on. The rain had torn away at its adhesive nature, but the black ink written on it was still clear.

Open it. It was a simple statement, but the phrase echoed his mind as he left the gas station. With Charlie trotting behind him, Patrick made a beeline toward his trunk. Now, the compartment smelled far worse than earlier.

"Damn your dirty laundry," he muttered. Patrick shoved one end of the crowbar beneath the trunk's door and pressed downward. He grunted as he put his entire weight on the object, and with one big breath, he leaped into the air, letting gravity use his entire body weight to pry open the vehicle. The sound of metal bending and groaning filled the air.

"Come on!" he yelled. Patrick shut his eyes and pushed harder. This time, his car croaked from the excessive pressure. "Open up!" He grunted one more time as the pressure on the crowbar came to a climax. With one more push, his shoulders tensed, his biceps grew larger, and his chest stung. But once the trunk broke open, and he loosened his grip, the world felt clearer, as though he had lifted a great weight from his chest.

He was about to smile, but soon, his lips turned into a frown as he peered into the pitch-black compartment. Although he didn't see everything, he saw a large garbage bag instead of Delan's clothes. He reached inside to grab ahold of whatever may be in there, but he quickly retracted his arm when he felt something soft, like skin. He gagged as dread consumed him. His fingers ran across the slender frame of whoever was inside.

"What the hell?" Patrick muttered. He glanced over his shoulder, afraid of exposing the contents, but Charlie growled at him. "I don't want to see it," he whispered. But instead of being the kind canine that he was, he bit down on Patrick's shin. "Fine!" He swatted a hand at Charlie, making him release his bite. He felt the presence of three other people entering the parking lot. The hairs on his neck stood up.

"I came here right after Delan died," a boy said. Patrick looked to his left, where his first doppelgänger stood. He appeared as dead as he was when he sat on the floor of the gas station. Except this time, the other two clones complimented his haggard appearance. The one from the cave stood still, with his mouth clenched. Meanwhile, the oldest version of himself stared into the trunk with a cigarette dangling from his mouth.

"Go on," he said plainly.

Patrick's eyes grew wide with fear. Charlie stared at him the same way Delan would when he begged for a new toy. Meanwhile, the others glared at him with a small tinge of sadness.

"Please, break the cycle," the one from the cave said. The others nodded in agreement.

Patrick reached deep into the compartment and wrapped his hands tightly around the top of the bag. He let out a large grunt and pulled out the bag, revealing the pale, stiff body of a woman inside. Patrick gasped and fell onto his rear.

"What the hell?" He turned around to face his doppelgangers, but they had disappeared again. Instead, it was just him and Charlie. The dog sniffed at the corpse and scratched the plastic bag with his paws. "Fine." Patrick gently untied the top and pulled it down, revealing Ms. Hawthorne's lifeless face. Thankfully, her eyelids remained shut, so he wouldn't have to see her soulless eyes staring at him.

Thunder struck in the distance, the dark clouds rolled over him, and soon, the sky darkened. Within that darkness, the pumps glowed, giving him enough vision to see around him. Patrick noticed the "open" sign flicker on, giving a red glow. But next to it was the name "Jay's Station."

Patrick looked down at Ms. Hawthorne's corpse.

"I don't get it," Patrick whispered.

A gust of wind blew behind him, and a gentle hand settled on his shoulder. "I want you to think. Remember what happened and accept the truth," Delan's voice spoke behind him.

Again, Patrick felt the urge to turn around, but he feared that just like before, his brother would disappear. For now, he'd have to revel in his touch one last time.

"I... I don't remember. You took your own life and then mine went downhill from there."

Delan's hand grew firmer, to where his nails dug into Patrick's skin. "Think again. Otherwise, you'll go through this same gas station again under the assumption of a life you never led."

Patrick shuddered as he touched an open wound on Ms. Hawthorne's side, making his memories return to him.

Chapter 23

Past

After their last session, Ms. Hawthorne stood proud, as if she were the greatest woman ever to live. In contrast, Patrick clutched his stomach, trying to hold down the vomit brewing in the depths of his stomach.

"Okay, can you help me now?" he asked.

Ms. Hawthorne nodded and examined the picture he left behind. She gave it another glance, and after a long pause, she set it down. "It was near the homecoming dance. That girl dyed her hair to match our school's colors," Ms. Hawthorne stated.

Patrick quietly nodded. "Can you give me anything else? I mean, who is she?"

Ms. Hawthorne shook her head. "There are hundreds of students who dye their hair like this. I'd be able to write an entire book filled with names."

Patrick jumped to his feet, feeling frustrated at being kept in the dark. "But there has to be something! It's getting closer to the end of the year! Isn't the yearbook already being made?"

Ms. Hawthorne opened her eyes wide at him, showing a hint of fear. "What are you planning?"

"If I can get a hold of the yearbook, I can look through the previous events held by the school. At least then I can find something."

Ms. Hawthorne shook her head. "No. You know our graphic design teacher and those students work hard to make that for us!"

"Well, it doesn't matter! I need to see what they see! If you won't help me get my hands on an early copy, then I'll do it myself!" Patrick stomped toward the doorway, only to be held back by Ms. Hawthorne's firm grip. She held his wrist like he was the last person in her life. But when he looked into her hollow eyes, he knew she only felt lust when cradling him.

"Why are you so scared?" he asked bluntly.

Ms. Hawthorne yelped, putting up a vulnerable demeanor.

"Because I'm worried about you. It's clear you're stressed. Why don't you stay here? We can spend the whole day releasing that stress?" A grin formed when the corners of her lips turned upward. She rested her hand on his chest and Patrick pushed her away.

She stumbled backward into the coat rack, knocking it over. "How could you? You hurt me!" She held the side of her face and gave a fake weeping.

Patrick bit down on the inside of his cheek questioning his actions. *She's not hurt. She's not hurt.* But no matter how much he told himself that, her sullen expression told him otherwise. In the end, he gave in and quietly said, "I'm sorry."

At his words, Ms. Hawthorne's face softened. She put her hand on his cheek again, showing that Patrick didn't leave a single mark on her skin. Nevertheless, he didn't point it out. "Are we okay? You and I." Before waiting for a response, she held on to him in a tight embrace. The same disturbance in his stomach returned.

"Yes," he mumbled.

"Good. One of the most important things about being an adult is being able to control your emotions. You want to be an adult, don't you?" She pulled back from her hug and ran her fingers through his hair. Patrick swallowed the urge to cry. He couldn't deny that she was correct to say that he wanted to be seen and treated as an adult, but the emotional turmoil he felt wasn't what he had in mind.

Patrick strode toward the door without hesitation. Ms. Hawthorne grabbed his arm once more, only to be shaken off. While she called out for him, Patrick drove back to school, ready to sneak into the graphic design class and snatch away all files and physical copies of the upcoming year book.

Once he arrived, the halls and courtyard were completely devoid of students, since classes were already in session. Patrick traversed the courtyard and noticed the substitute teacher, who often filled in for Ms. Hawthorne, walking through the campus. He cursed the school for having three separate buildings. He slipped past the benches and vending machines, avoiding all faculty members, and luckily reached the farthest building without being caught.

He entered it, leaving behind the cool air. While he traversed the wide corridors covered by stone floors, he continuously looked over his shoulder to make sure he wasn't being watched. He scooted along the wall and peeked his head around the corner to peer in through the tiny window of the door. With the classroom fully devoid of students, Patrick figured that the teacher must have been spending her time in the lounge enjoying her lunch break or took the current period to plan out a lesson.

He gently pulled downward on the handle and allowed himself in without making a noise. Patrick looked past the rows of cubicles harboring many computers that students used to create digital art. With quick strides, he ran to the back of the classroom, where the teacher's desk waited for him. He quickly pulled out every single drawer, scouring it for flash drives, photos, and notes. Without knowing what each piece held, Patrick shoved as much as he could into his pockets. After stealing two flash drives and a notebook which he clung to his chest, he attempted to log into the teacher's computer. But just as he was about to do so, he lifted his head at the sound of someone walking through the halls. Patrick duck beneath the desk, praying that the person would simply pass, but much to his dismay, he heard them open the door.

Patrick crawled beneath the desk and held his breath. The person slammed what sounded like a large backpack onto a table in one of the cubicles. He crawled out from the desk and crouched behind the short walls, housing each office space. He listened intently to the intruder.

In a short time, Patrick walked around the perimeter of the classroom without getting caught. Upon nearing the door, he saw the individual was a girl who spent the entire time staring at her phone screen. Patrick gulped hard, knowing that despite not seeing him, she'd hear the door open. Still, he feared that someone else would barge in at any moment. So, while the screen occupied her, Patrick quickly burst through the door, making sure to face away from her.

"Who's there?" he heard her say as he scampered down the hallway. Patrick ran toward the exit, fingering the items he shoved in his pockets while the notebook slowly contorted into odd angles as he held it in a death grip. But once he was finally outside, he took a moment to breathe before hopping over the gates of the school and making his way back to his car.

When he finally entered his vehicle, Patrick breathed a sigh of relief, knowing that he finally found the evidence he needed, and that perhaps his investigation may end sooner than he expected. He excitedly drove home while formulating another plan in his head. He decided that he'd first look at the flash drives to determine if there was anything of interest. Afterward, he'd scour the notebook and copy the notes onto his own sheet of paper. And now, for the first time since Delan's suicide attempt, Patrick felt a tinge of hope. He looked in the rear-view mirror and smiled.

"Delan, I love you," he whispered. He pictured his brother in the backseat of his car, knowing Delan would have loved the heartfelt proclamation, but for now, Patrick would have to wait until the hospital discharged his brother.

When Patrick finally returned to his house, he saw his parents were already home. With their car parked in the driveway, Patrick knew it was time for him to apologize to his mother. That reminder stirred a deep-rooted sense of anxiety within him, an anxiety that breathing exercises couldn't quell. Although he never got along with his mother because of her temper, he knew his father was right to scold his behavior. So, the moment he rested his hand on the doorknob, he braced himself to face the consequences of his actions.

"Mom," Patrick said as soon as he opened the door. However, a rain cloud suddenly cast over his head when he realized both his parents were crying. "Dad?" He looked at his father's ashen face.

"Patrick, have a seat so we can talk." The man spoke calmly, despite the overwhelming number of tears forming in his eyes. He gestured for Patrick to take a chair, but when he stood still in utter confusion, his mother made him jump when she knocked a glass off the table.

"Do what he says!" she yelled.

After her outburst, Patrick's father gently shushed her and kissed her forehead. "I understand you're upset, but please, let's talk this out." He rocked her in his arms, but her facial expression told Patrick that she was hesitant.

He carefully approached the dining table and sat beside his weeping mother. "What's going on?" he asked nervously.

His dad coughed to clear his throat before fixing his collar. "Delan is dead," he said bluntly. The moment he ended his sentence, his mother wailed as though his brother dropped to the ground at their feet. "We got the news this afternoon while we were at the hospital."

Patrick stumbled and placed his hand on the table to keep himself steady. The cloth beneath his skin wrinkled as he tightened his grip. "How? You said he only threatened to kill himself! You didn't say he tried to." Patrick placed his hands on the sides of his face as he hyperventilated.

His dad took a seat. "During an arts and crafts therapy session, he hid one paintbrush before they cleaned the area. Afterward, he broke the handle and used it to . . ." His dad stopped speaking when Patrick put his hands over his ears. Patrick wondered what went through Delan's head. The amount of determination it must have taken to end his life in such a manner haunted him. Soon, brutal images of his little brother filled his head like a parasite.

His mother covered her mouth, turning her cry into a muffled scream. "And where have you been?" she asked accusingly.

Patrick flinched when her finger pointed at his face. "I-I've." He wanted to confess everything. To blurt out that he had been trying to find the girl responsible for causing so much grief, but the disappointment in his parent's face made him queasy. Not only that, but the things he did with Ms. Hawthorne disgusted him.

I should've focused on him. Only him . . . His throat tightened to keep the words from spilling out of his mouth.

"So, you have nothing to say? Your brother is dead, and you haven't been by our side at all!" His mother stood from her chair, leaned over, and grabbed Patrick by his collar. "Do you have any idea how much this hurts?"

Tears welled in the corners of her eyes. "Hold on," his dad said comfortingly. He held her hands to steady them. "We'll talk about this later. As one family."

Patrick's mom shook her head before standing up and slowly walking to her room. Her head hung low while she muttered incoherently beneath her breath. Once the door slammed shut, Patrick fidgeted uncomfortably in his chair. Only then did his dad sit across from him and began crying profusely.

"Dad, I- I'm sorry. I . . ."

The man continued to cry for the next few minutes. "To be honest, I don't know what to say. I'm winging my entire way through this thing. I don't know how to talk to you or your mother!" he raised his voice, yet not a single hint of anger lingered. Instead, Patrick only saw pain and helplessness. "For now, I think it's best we spend a couple of hours to ourselves. Then we can get together later."

He lay back in his chair without watching Patrick leave the room.

The moment Patrick escaped to his bedroom, he quietly shut the door behind him and angrily slammed the flash drive into the front panel of his computer. Upon turning his desktop on, a message popped up from Khen, which he ignored entirely.

He needed to know who the girl was so he could take his revenge. He clicked on the folder that popped up when inserting the USB. All photographs were neatly organized by dates. Patrick immediately went to the beginning of the year, where he consciously scanned every person he saw.

After the first three pictures, he didn't notice anyone with the dyed hair that Ms. Hawthorne claimed "every girl did." Patrick grew more and more agitated.

His emotion soon turned into grief when he saw his brother in more photos. Each one showed him happy, but by the start of the second month of the school year, his mouth slowly turned into a frown. But most surprising of all, Ms. Hawthorne made more appearances. In one photo, she and his brother stood with the entire classroom. The woman looked at him like he was a precious puppy. But as the weeks went by, Patrick noticed her face contort into the same haughty look she gave him.

After a few more slides, his brother was completely sullen, and then Patrick's heart raced when he noticed the following pictures depicting decorations marking the arrival of the homecoming dance.

Of course, other students displayed their school's colors but only through their clothing. It wasn't until the next picture that Patrick became frozen in place. He leaned in, making sure that he was seeing everything correctly. *That can't be . . .* Standing in a sea of students was Ms. Hawthorne, smiling at the camera with dyed hair. Her golden locks were black with red streaks in them.

Patrick quickly went through the rest of the pictures, hoping that perhaps a female student had the same hair dye, but once he shuffled through every file, he realized that only Ms. Hawthorne fit the description.

Patrick slammed his fist on the keyboard, feeling like an idiot. The world around him swirled as he realized how stupid he was.

Delan, I'm so sorry. He jumped from his chair and pushed open his door with a thunderous bang. Afterward, he marched down the stairs past his grieving father and drove toward his teacher's house.

Chapter 24

The Past

On the way to Ms. Hawthorne's residence, rain clouds formed in the sky, darkening it as though the rapture began. But through it all, Patrick only felt rage. He didn't care what he said to her, as long as she was punished. After his tires spun through the wet ground, he parked his car in front of her driveway to block her vehicle. He stomped toward her doorway as the rain soaked his skin.

He waited patiently for her to answer the door. His ears picked-up on every little sound from his heartbeat to the way the raindrops hit his car.

"Ms. Hawthorne." He knocked. For a moment, he shut his eyes and whispered to himself, "Delan, forgive me for what I'm going to do." After he finished, he opened his eyes to see Ms. Hawthorne standing at the front door with a smile on her face.

"Come inside," she said cheerfully. She let Patrick in and shut the door. "How are you?" she asked, turning him around. Her smile quickly faded upon seeing his stone face. "Jesus, what's wrong?"

Rather than answering her, Patrick leaned in and gave her a kiss. The act made him want to pull away and hide in a corner, but it was enough to let her guard down. When she closed her eyes and gave into his long kiss, her shoulders relaxed.

"How about you have a seat on the couch?" he suggested.

"It's about time you take the initiative." She giggled to herself. When she plopped onto the sofa, Patrick slowly walked toward the kitchen, stopping in front of the knife set.

"Is it just me?" he asked.

"What do you mean?"

Patrick watched her confused expression within the reflection of the steel toaster. "Am I the only one you've been having sex with?"

Ms. Hawthorne nodded. "Of course!"

Patrick shook his head and discreetly fingered the handle of one of the blades. "Don't lie to me." His voice grew coarse, as though his throat turned into sandpaper. He eyed Ms. Hawthorne's reflection once more.

She took a moment to answer. "You mean the world to me. I'd never cheat on you."

Patrick scoffed. "Did you also act nice to my brother before you raped him?" He turned around with the knife in his hand. He brandished the blade, making sure the light would clearly illuminate it. A tear escaped his eye as he fought back the urge to jump at her.

"Patrick, what are you doing?" she asked with a trembling voice.

Her lips quivered the same way his mother's did when she cried. And once Ms. Hawthorne gradually stood from her seat, she held her hands up.

"I looked at the images from the homecoming dance. You said almost every girl had dyed hair, but you were the only one who dyed your hair! You were the one who stood close to Delan! You were the one who got happier as he got more miserable!"

He pointed the tip of the knife at her.

"Patrick, please stop," she whispered.

He smacked a mug off the counter and walked toward her.

"Shut up and answer me!"

She screamed and ran around the other end of the coffee table. She placed the furniture in between them with her eye darting toward the front door.

"Don't bother running. You know I'm faster than you."

Ms. Hawthorne held her breath.

"I never hurt Delan!" she screeched and kicked the table forward. The edges struck Patrick's knees, making him buckle over. Afterward, she sprinted past him into her garage. Patrick heard her press the button to open the garage door. He quickly stumbled to her location, noticing the fear in her eyes, when she realized he blocked her car with his.

"Please stop!" she said. Patrick put his hand over her mouth and dragged her inside the house. He threw her on the ground and locked themselves inside.

"Just answer my question. What did you do to him?"

Ms. Hawthorne sniffled for a few moments until she hardened her gaze. "Okay, I had sex with him. There, you happy now?"

She jumped to her feet and pushed him against the door. Patrick stood motionless, trying to take in what she said.

"That's right, I fucked him the same way I did to you! But here's the thing, it wasn't just me he had a problem with. It was you, too."

She reached for the kitchen cabinet above her head and pulled out a black journal. She opened it and held it in her hands, reading numerous passages, many of which criticized Patrick's actions throughout the year.

"See this? These are things Delan said about you! The little brat writes too much, so I took this." She grinned and read a passage while mocking his brother's voice. "'He's the first one I thought of opening up to, but with the way he looks at those girls, I'm afraid he'll give me a pat on the back. That he'll congratulate me for 'bagging' Ms. Hawthorne, or worse, he'll get jealous and cut me off.'"

After reading, she shut the journal and glared at Patrick before stepping closer to him. "Delan saw you as a monster. He felt betrayed by who you became." Her words dripped out of her mouth like venom.

Patrick tightened his hold on the knife handle. The emotions bubbling inside him were ready to burst, and he couldn't contain them any longer.

He lowered his voice and spoke once more.

"You killed my brother. That's the only reason I need to kill you." After his threat, Ms. Hawthorne's eyes grew wide. She slapped him, but he responded by tackling her. And as she lay on her back, mortified, Patrick raised the blade high in the air. With his other hand, he covered her mouth.

"We're both horrible people," he said softly. Afterward, she screamed into his palm as he thrust the knife downward into her abdomen. Patrick cried to himself as he finished the job, leaving her as nothing more than a corpse with a mutilated torso. He stood and searched every cabinet for a garbage bag. When he found one, he stripped Ms. Hawthorne of all her clothing and stuffed her body inside the sealed plastic. He made a sloppy knot to hold it together.

Afterward, he tossed her clothes into the fireplace, lit the match set he found from her kitchen, and watched the flames devour her belongings. Patrick felt a great weight lift from his chest, only to be replaced by another. He let out a hysterical sobbing fit.

I'm sorry. Not only did he want to hug Delan and apologize for everything he'd done, but he wanted to do the same for his parents as well. He knew he passed the point of no return and that tonight, they'd lost both of their sons. As he dragged Ms. Hawthorne to the trunk of his car, he thought of his mother and how broken she'd be, as well as the stress his father would go through. The vision of the man trying to keep himself together and what remained of his family told Patrick that he put the kindest father in the world into a permanent hell.

He heaved the corpse into his trunk and shut it tightly, only to cry what little emotions remained.

"Mom, Dad . . ." He took in a deep breath and entered his car. "I'm so sorry," he whispered. His trembling hand reached for the glove compartment where he examined all the memorabilia he stored. He glossed over the postcard from an old vacation, as well as the flip lighter his grandfather passed down to him. Patrick shut his eyes, letting a tear drop steadily slide down his cheek.

This is it. He let out a deep breath, knowing that his life was over. So, from then on, he drove at the speed limit toward the outskirts of town, eventually arriving at the same gas station he sought refuge at during the bonfire. As he sat in the parking lot, the skies darkened and his vision became gray as a deep fog consumed him.

The world around him dissipated as the radio became his only friend.

"Welcome to Twin Peaks," a woman's voice said. Patrick turned down the dial, but her voice still spoke loudly through the speakers. "Admit your sins and seek the truth," the woman said ominously.

Chapter 24

PRESENT

As Patrick recollected his memories, the rain lightened until it completely stopped. Soon, the fog rolled away, revealing a clear blue sky. He put Ms. Hawthorne's body back into the trunk and shut it. Upon staring out at the lake, he realized just how beautiful it was. The fresh smell of the rain combined with the glistening water made the place look like it was heaven. And as he stared past the railing, he saw the remnants of the bonfire. Patrick got inside his car and found Charlie already waiting for him in the passenger's seat. The dog let his tongue hang loose as Patrick pulled away from the station.

He went uphill, his wheels grinding against the muddy slope. Patrick stomped hard on the gas to get through the sludge, and as they reached the top, the view of the small town of Twin Peaks revealed itself. His eyes opened wide at the narrow streets, city center, and residential areas. All of it resembled every American town he saw on television. Had he stumbled upon this place before, never would he have guessed that it was a ghost town.

The road brought him downward and as he entered, he observed various men in robes standing nearby. They watched Patrick cruise over the road in silence. Charlie growled at the window, baring his teeth at the strangers.

"I remember when I first came here," a gruff voice said. Instantly, Patrick knew the oldest of the doppelgangers had reappeared in his car.

He peered over his shoulder at the hardened man, who finally seemed a little more relaxed.

"I went to the gas station, planning to refuel my car before going on another case. I thought these guys were the criminals I was supposed to catch." The man sighed and leaned back in his seat. "It's strange to drive by them again. Don't you feel like an animal in a zoo right now?"

Patrick ignored him and continued forward. Images of the town flickered in his head. He recalled the first time he arrived, and re-membered standing in a blizzard rather than the thunderstorm. He remembered how he stumbled upon the massive hotel at the center of the city. Patrick flinched and put a hand to his forehead.

"I felt a lot of pain when the memories came back, too." His other self leaned his head against the window, watching the men in robes gather on the sides of the street. "We're here." He pointed to the towers staring down at them. Patrick watched his reflection in the rear-view mirror. The way he ran his finger across the air reminded him of the look he always gave his parents when getting lost in his imagination.

Patrick parked the car and stepped outside. Charlie followed him, still growling and baring his teeth at the men in brown robes. Patrick rubbed the top of his head as he ushered him toward the front door.

"I'm ready," he muttered to himself. Afterward, he entered the building. First, everything went black. He listened to Charlie panting beside him. Soon, the flicker of a lighter sounded in the distance. A few more strikes were made until a small orange flame illuminated Dabria, who sat on a couch in front of him.

"Take a seat," she said. Charlie turned his attention to her, and she spoke to the animal. "I understand we're still on bad terms, but please, settle down for Patrick's sake." At her request, Charlie sat down next to the armchair behind Patrick. After Dabria made another gesture, Patrick took the armchair. The cushion engulfed him and he eased himself into the furniture. "In each of your lives, you relished that chair," she observed casually. "Now, I assume you found out the truth, correct?"

Patrick nodded. He looked to Dabria's left, where Luke stood. holding a candle. He dawned the same brown robes as the others. "Hello," he said awkwardly.

Dabria raised her hand to silence him.

"I'm afraid you still need more training for how to converse with others."

"I am terribly sorry," he said. He gave a slight bow, which she waved off. "There's no need to apologize. After all, you are one of my most loyal followers."

"Thank you," Luke said. He stifled his voice as though holding back a tear. "Your compliment means the world to me. I will—"

"Please, give me some time to talk to our guest."

Luke nodded and went back to standing silently.

"What's all of this?" Patrick asked.

"First, you tell me what you've discovered."

Patrick eyed her and his body stiffened. Charlie nuzzled himself closer to him, acting as a protector.

"I killed my teacher. I killed Ms. Hawthorne."

Dabria nodded. "So, here we are again."

"Yes, but I don't have all of my memories back," Patrick said flatly.

"I would assume so. It's amazing how deeply your lies have affected you. I've had many unique individuals enter my realm. All of you try so hard to deny your sins, but you were different. I've never seen anyone so delusional before."

Patrick swallowed the lump in his throat. "Tell me, which parts of Twin Peaks do you control?"

Dabria smirked. "I merely decide who comes in and who goes out. The rest is born from your imagination."

Patrick squinted his eyes. "I don't understand."

Dabria smirked once more. "To put it simply, this town feeds off of you. It uses your biggest fears and disappointments to inflict pain. You see yourself as a monster, correct?"

Patrick nodded, thinking about the doppelgangers once more, and soon his mind ventured to his brother. Of course, he was the most important person in the world, but at the same time, his journal had put more than guilt into Patrick's heart. He hated to say it, but he feared Delan. He feared the way his little brother felt toward him, and that anxiety rooted itself deeply into Patrick's chest.

Looking back, the image of himself he tried so hard to show his peers felt like nothing. He only wished he could be the big brother Delan deserved.

"I see the pain in your face," Dabria said. "I suppose this cycle has ended."

Patrick nodded. "I don't want to live as a monster."

Dabria raised an eyebrow. "Don't tell me you plan to push yourself further into delusion." She spoke sarcastically, ready to belittle him some more.

But Patrick merely shook his head. "No, I'll accept what I am, but I . . ." He couldn't find the strength to finish his sentence.

"Very well then." Dabria motioned for Luke to come forward. She whispered in his ear, prompting him to pull Patrick up by the arm. In doing so, he agitated Charlie, who began barking violently. "Settle down, you mutt!" Dabria yelled. "You and I have fought before, but now we have a deal. You guide the souls that come here, and in return, I keep myself in line. I won't hurt him and none of my followers will either."

Charlie gave her a long stare.

"I keep my promises," she said. "After all, Sofia was the last person I met, and we both know how that ended." She pointed to the burn scar on her face. Afterward, Luke escorted Patrick to the entrance, where a blinding white light bombarded them once they opened the door.

Within seconds, Patrick found himself alone in his car. With no one in sight, he took in his surroundings. The sky was sunny, giving him a clear view of the lake. Meanwhile, once he looked to his right, he noticed a different employee standing at the gas station. It was the same grumpy man that let him use his phone the night Patrick escaped the party.

The backseat remained empty. Delan's clothes were completely gone, and the journal that Ms. Hawthorne took waited in the seat next to him. Her blood still stained the cover, seeping into the pages within. Patrick looked down, noticing the kitchen knife soaked in blood. For a moment, he wondered if he was still in Twin Peaks, so he left his vehicle and went toward the station.

"Hello," he said as he opened the door.

The man sighed. "You again? What do you want?"

Patrick gave a nervous smile. "Could I use your phone?"

The man rolled his eyes. "Fine, but if you come here again, I won't hesitate to kick you out." He tossed his device and Patrick caught it, gently cradling it in his hands.

He quickly dialed his mother's phone number. As he held it against his ear, his foot tapped nervously.

"Hello?" his mom asked.

Patrick steadied himself before talking.

"Hi, Mom." He shut his eyes, expecting her to berate him, but instead, she cried. It was a genuine cry. One that held both anger and sadness. The same mixture only his mother could do, and that's when he knew he was back in the real world. "I love you," he said.

"Hold on." After a beep, he heard his father's voice as well. He realized his mother put him on speaker. "I'm sorry I yelled at you. Please, come home," she pleaded.

"That's right. Both of us want to see you again," his dad said. As usual, he used a gentle tone, but Patrick could tell he was on the verge of tears.

"I'm sorry, but I can't."

"Why?" his mom asked.

Patrick looked over to the lake, imagining himself at the very bottom of it. But rather than explaining anything to his parents, he only made one last statement. "I'm sorry."

"Wait—"

He hung up the phone before his father could finish his sentence. When Patrick handed the device back to the cashier, he looked away. Quickly, Patrick strode to his car and gently dropped the notebook and knife onto the ground. Next, he opened his trunk and dumped Ms. Hawthorne's body next to everything else.

"They'll know what you did," Patrick muttered. He returned to the driver's seat and started the ignition. His engine revved quietly as he took a deep breath.

"Delan, I love you." He waited a moment, wishing that he were still in Twin Peaks, so his brother would reveal himself. But when he heard nothing, except for his heart beating over the silence, he looked forward. "I will not live as a monster," he whispered to himself.

Patrick stomped the gas pedal, transforming his car into a missile shooting through the metal railing and into the lake. He shivered as the freezing water traveled up to his chest. He felt himself sinking faster and faster until he was completely submerged. Once the water consumed him, he slammed his hand down on the seatbelt, hoping to keep himself from struggling out of it, but naturally, his body fought hard. While the water clogged his lungs, he jerked side to side, sending his limbs into a frenzy. But after the sunlight seeped through his windshield, he felt warm for a few seconds, until the loss of consciousness gave him peace.

Hello Dear Reader,

I have a confession to make. While this novel is largely fiction, I drew many events, characters, and experiences from my life and the lives of others I've met. I won't go into great detail for the sake of privacy, but just know that you are loved, and you matter.

Best regards,

Danie Santos

Please join me so that we can share stories such as this to touch the hearts of many.

https://dashboard.mailerlite.com/forms/1107901/1333163363286 39826/share